Darklings

Darklings

Scott Cirakovic

Copyright © 2026 by Scott Cirakovic
All rights reserved. No part of this book may be reproduced in any manner whatsoever without written permission except in the case of brief quotations embodied in critical articles and reviews.
First Printing, 2026

Contents

Dedication		vii
1	Duty	1
2	Pain	7
3	Addiction	15
4	Lust	28
5	Vengeance	37
6	Vengeance	48
7	Lust	58
8	Pain	68
9	Vengeance	75
10	Addiction	87
11	Lust	96
12	Pain	103

13	Vengeance	113
14	Lust	121
15	Retribution	134
16	Duty	146

About the Author 161

For all those who fight to stay good in an increasingly dark world.

1

Duty

The boy watched in silence as his master stood, his robe billowing out as he stepped towards the stone table. Placing the book down with a thud, his master turned and spoke, voice soft and yet no less powerful for it.

'Do you feel it, Septimus?'

Septimus nodded. It had been impossible to miss; like ice had filled his veins, scouring him from the inside out. Throughout all his training, his master had warned him that this day was coming, that this was their destiny, that they had been chosen to stand firm before the darkness. In that moment though, he only felt fear.

'I'm afraid,' he admitted, voice soft.

His master, the venerable Praetores, champion of the Weavers of Fate, smiled down at him, white beard lit by the soft orange glow of the flame. 'So am I.'

The admission shook him. Septimus had never considered that his master could feel base emotions such as fear.

Surely someone who wielded the power etherium, who was its master, could not feel fear. Maybe that only counted when facing mortal foes.

Praetores stepped over to the fire, burning in the stone fireplace, the chimney carved with intricate gargoyles. Those faces had once given him nightmares. Now, they were as comforting as an old blanket. This room had been the centre of his life. Fulfilling his duties out of habit, he stood from his own high-backed chair, closing the book he had been studying, and picked up his master's. Stacking the book on his own, he stepped over to the large oak bookshelf and carefully slid them both into place. There was a sad sense of finality to the ritual. Septimus looked around the room, trying to memorise the stone walls, the worn rug in the centre, the stone benches with various half-complete experiments and dirty alembics. It was comfortably cluttered.

'You know which direction you must go?' his master asked.

Septimus took the proffered cloak, flicking it over his shoulders, and nodded. 'I can feel the pull.'

'Of course you can.' Another smile, although this time the sadness was obvious.

'Is there no other way?'

'You know there is not.' His master rebuked him softly.

He still had dim memories of a master that was not soft and kind. Of a cane that bit harshly into his skin, shouted curses, and hunger. That was not his master's way though.

Septimus sighed.

'The path we have been chosen to walk is not an easy one, Septimus. Have I ever lied to you about our duty? Have I not given you the opportunity to leave and forge your own path?'

His cheeks flushed hot. 'You've never lied to me master.' He gripped his staff tight, knuckles turning white. For the first time, he noticed that he was almost as tall as his master, who suddenly looked old and frail. The white beard was no longer a sign of wisdom but of age. 'I just wish…' he trailed off and looked at his feet.

'There is no shame in your wish. I too wish it. The Allmother cannot touch the well, just as she cannot directly touch those of us who wield etherium. Through her prophets we are set on our path, to do her will even as we are damned to endure the absence of her voice.'

Septimus looked into his masters twinkling blue eyes and knew he spoke the truth. The look firmed his resolve.

'We have a duty to fulfill.'

His master nodded, smile returning. 'That we do. Remember, once the well of power shifts, you must find its vessel before the enemy. Its pull has already begun, which means the Allmother is finally moving within the realm of mortals once again. The Weavers of Fate must stand ready.'

Those words repeated through his mind as they departed, his master turning left down the path in front of the tower, Septimus turning right. He did not look back. It was still dark but there was enough moonlight to see by, and he didn't need to resort to his power for sight. For several hours he marched, letting his mind wander, not wanting to think about what was happening. Topping a rise in the mountains, he looked out across the valley.

His breath caught.

A fog bank was washing in with the coming of dawn. But this was no normal fog. It shimmered strangely. A pink glow was emanating from one of the cliffs which he knew to be the entrance to the well of power both he and his master were sworn to defend. Or at least, they had been. That particular duty was about to be complete. Power pulsed, the pink glow from the pool bathing the rocks around the cave entrance, the swirling fog glowing as it approached the cliff. A shadow appeared on top of the cliff, a sole figure of a man, cloaked and holding a staff as he faced the approaching fog.

The power pulsed from the cave.

Tears rolled down his cheeks. A figure was emerging from the fog bank, still little more than fog itself, but gaining corporeal form. It was as large as the cliff, if not larger. Once fully formed, its horned head would be level with his master on top of the cliff, taloned hands large enough to squash Praetores with a single grip.

Septimus cried.

And then he fled, young feet taking him swiftly from his home forever, leaving his master to his fate.

He didn't see the flash of pink light behind him as the well's power pulsed a final time, etherium of the Allmother freed from its cradle to seek out its chosen one.

Septimus ran.

He had a duty to perform.

He was the last surviving Weaver of Fate.

2

Pain

Claws scratched in the dark, pulling at him, trying to slow him.

Pain.

Fire across his cheek.

He wiped at it, the blood hot on his frozen fingers.

Scrabbling. Scrabbling in the dark.

Forward.

Have to keep moving forward.

Pain.

Stabbing pain in his knees and shins. This was not a new pain though. This was one of the many pains that accompanied him through life. It told him he was still alive. Surely, if he was to join the Allmother, his pains would be washed away. Wouldn't they?

Don't think about that. Just keep moving forward.

Silver moonlight broke through the canopy for just a moment, but not soon enough for him to see the tree root. His legs were leaden. His mind sluggish. His reactions too slow.

Pain.

Burning in his palms. Back pinching. Stink of wet soil filled his nostrils. The moist foliage of the forest floor soaking into his already soiled shirt, empty weapons belt digging into his stomach.

Get up old man!

'Get up!' His voice was scratchy and raw. Just another pain.

He groaned. Muscles protesting as he forced them to work. A different type of pain, the type that came from a hard fight or a long day's labour.

Move it, soldier!

The moonlight disappeared behind the trees again.

Scrabbling in the dark.

Time lost all meaning in the blackness. Minutes. Seconds. Hours. All the same. Just endless pain stretching forward into the abyss.

His body reacted before conscious thought had time to form. He rolled as it hit him, his hearing telling him of the threat a second before it struck. Aching muscles worked, years of drills and training tensing and relaxing just the right ones.

Pain.

A sharp pain in his shoulder. The combined weight of him and his attacker awoke the old tear.

His muscles worked and he found himself on top of his wriggling opponent.

Fists clenched. Third knuckle aching. A broken bone in a bar fight almost twenty years ago and yet the pain was still there.

The squeal stopped him. His fist hovered in the dark.

Darklings don't squeal.

His heart pounded in his ears. Even after all this time, after the training, the battles, his heart pounded. *Traitorous bastard of an organ.*

'Allmother.' Barely a whisper, but he heard it.

Darklings don't talk.

'Human?' he asked, voice barely louder than the whisper of the wind through the trees.

A whimper. Then a word. 'Ye ... yes.'

He unclenched his fist, pain easing in his finger joints, only to be replaced by the pain in his knees as he eased himself off the man beneath him. It was an old pain though; one he could ignore.

The clouds shifted above them, letting another stream of moonlight to bathe the men in its cool light.

Just a boy, he realised. *Barely older than he would be now if ...*

Pain.

The worst kind.

Don't follow that thought anymore. Must survive.

'We need to move lad,' he said, holding out a hand to him. His fear receded a touch; not much, but enough.

'Who are you?' His voice broke slightly.

'Oswald.'

'From the outpost?'

'Yes.'

'Then maybe others -'

'No,' he hissed, grabbing the boy by the shoulder. His own shoulder stabbed with pain at the sudden movement. 'We need to move lad. Darklings move fast and can see in the dark, unlike us.'

He shoved the boy forward and lumbered back into motion.

The claws scratched at his face again.

His breath frosted as he ran, the cold burning his lungs. A searing pain to counterpoint his aches. The lad wheezed along behind him, the only indication that he was still there, the endless dark having closed around them again.

Keep moving old man, don't let their sacrifice be for nothing.

Scrabbling. Scrabbling in the dark. Ignore the pain.

'I can't,' the lad wheezed, pawing weakly at his shoulder. 'Oswald!'

'Keep moving.'

'It hurts.'

'That's life.'

He slowed but kept moving. The boy stopped.

'Don't leave me,' the boy whimpered. 'I don't want to be alone in the dark.'

Oswald paused. His muscles ached. Lungs burned. Pain. Even when still, pain was his companion.

'Alone in the dark is exactly what I hope we are.'

He took another step. It took all his willpower to get moving again. The cold was sapping the heat from his body quicker than he had expected, his muscles cooling and going tight.

'What was that?' the lad asked.

Kid's jumping at shadows.

He wondered if he was any better.

Bracing himself for the pain, he was about to tell the lad to shut up and move. Instead, he heard what the lad had heard.

Ticking.

The noise that mandibles clacking together make.

The sound of death.

'Run!' he bellowed.

The pain was nothing. The fear was everything.

He ran, scrabbling in the dark, heart pounding in his ears.

Screams. Screams in the dark. A boy's scream of pure fear echoing through the trees that once again were trying to slow him down, to stop him.

His wet shirt chafed under his arms, but he didn't notice. His knees and shins ached with the old pain, but he didn't notice. The pain in his shoulder stabbed at him, but he didn't notice.

A moonlit clearing opened up before him in the dark. Even the promise of that small light made his heart swell with hope. He ran. He ran and tried to ignore the sound of branches breaking behind him.

A giant redwood stood in the centre of the clearing, its branches creating a circle of darkness in the centre of light.

He didn't stop. He ran through the moonlit clearing towards the tree, his only hope of sanctuary was likely high in its branches.

Can darklings climb?

There was no scrabbling now, just a mad dash through the cold night. The pain was there, but distant. He knew the lad was no longer behind him, but that was a pain he had no time for just then.

Only a few steps now. A few steps and he would be under the redwood branches.

A weight hit him in the centre of the back. He put out his hands to stop his fall, waiting for the pain ...

Only, there was no pain.

The grass was warm and soft underneath him, almost welcoming him to slumber. The biting cold was gone, his fingers no longer tingling with cold. But the pain.

No.

There was no pain.

He lifted his head and blinked, eyes adjusting to the warm orange light all around him. Blinking twice, his eyes went wide as he pushed himself to his knees. For the first time in what felt like a lifetime, he didn't groan at the movement or cringe at the thought of being on his knees.

The giant redwood tree was still before him, only now it was larger, its green leaves glowing and bathing him in the orange light. There was no sun, just the light of the tree.

'How?' he muttered to himself. 'Where?'

Standing, he stumbled towards the base of the glowing redwood. He glanced around but saw nothing. Everything outside the tree's light was an abyss, a darkness in which the pain lived. There was nothing there he wanted.

A figure stood at the base of the tree before him. He knew it was a female but could not make out more than that. She was bathed in the tree's light, barely a handful of steps before him, and yet he did not see her. As if his mind could not comprehend her beauty.

Roses. Roses and wild berries. The smell washed over him, mixed with an undertone of pure, clean earth. It was intoxicating. He breathed deep, eyes closed as euphoria rushed through his veins.

'Allmother,' he whispered.

'Oswald.'

It was a voice that said his name, and yet it wasn't. It was as if the very air knew him and acknowledged him, simply by being around him.

Exhaustion overcame him like a wave crashing on the rocks. His strength gave out and it was all he could do to lower himself to the soft green grass. He looked up at the glowing leaves, letting their glow wash over him before letting himself sink into oblivion.

Pain.

The pain awoke him.

Oswald groaned. The grass was cold and wet underneath him, his fingers aching and back throbbing. Rolling over to a sitting position was agony, but he managed it, a sheen of sweat on his forehead despite the cold.

The sun was coming up.

His night of terror was over. *Darklings don't hunt during the day.*

He laughed. Oswald laughed until tears streamed down his face and it turned to sobs.

Ignore the pain old man, he said to himself. *Don't let their deaths be for nothing.*

The sun rose above the horizon. Oswald stood. He ignored the dried blood all around where he had awoken. It may have been his, once, but that didn't matter anymore. He just had to push through the pain.

The fate of the outpost needed to be told. The Order needed to hear of it and only he remained to tell the tale.

'Allmother watch over me.' He looked up at the branches of the redwood tree, but its leaves did not glow. 'Accept me back to your embrace once my task is complete.'

Pain.

He started running.

Pain.

He would share his pain with the darklings. His physical pain was the least of it. Oswald was used to the physical pain. It was the other, worse pain that he would share.

And he had so much to share.

3

Addiction

Shaking hands.

Always with the shaking hands. It wasn't just from hunger this time. She needed a fix, and she knew it. The only problem was she had no money to score a fix with.

I could try to rob the distro, she thought to herself, dismissing it just as quickly. The distro's who sell the seraphim always have guards, even if you can't always see them lurking around. She'd heard that the distro on the east side had a shade as a guard. It may not be true, but it wasn't worth the risk... not yet anyway.

She rubbed her hands on the tattered skirt of her dress, ignoring the holes that were slowly growing in it.

The emptiness was growing inside of her, the pit opening its maws.

A stone on the dirt road stabbed her shoeless foot, sending a lance of pain up her leg. She winced but otherwise ignored it. What was pain when compared to the emptiness inside of her?

Gotta get a purse today, she told herself desperately. Two days without any successes. She knew her once desirable figure was turning to flesh and bones, meaning her earnings from selling it were rapidly diminishing. The first time she had bedded down with a man her earnings had kept her supplied for a week. Now, she could barely entice them. Absently, she toyed with the idea of spending her next purse on a bath and some new clothes. Maybe then she could make some more money from taking men to bed.

That would mean longer before I can see the distro, her second voice told her. Shaking wracked her at the thought. Her second voice was right, she couldn't wait that long.

Moving slowly down the street, she kept her shoulders hunched and head down. The afternoon crowd was thick around the market, making the air dusty and close which she hated. It made her feel trapped in a press of people. Like a fat man was groaning and flopping on top of her. She wouldn't bed another fat man. She had promised herself as much after the last one that sweated all over her. The second voice inside whispered about the coin she could make but she ignored it … for now.

The stone buildings sapped the sunlight around her. Even on a warm sunny day like today, Zailhiem was a grey and dreary place. Once a military outpost, it had become a trading town after the Graphim Empire was defeated and the need for a military presence was gone. There were still city guard -

she had developed almost a sense for when they were around - but no soldiers.

She shuffled through the crowd, doing her best to be unassuming as she moved with the flow.

Rich if plain cloak, soft hands with multiple rings, well-groomed hair. As simple as that, her target was marked.

The young merchant stopped at a fruit grocer's stall and haggled over a small bundle of apples. She slowed her step, blending with the crowd rather than trying to stop somewhere and look unassuming. Once that may have worked, but not now. Not with the way she looked. It was better to keep moving. Pain lanced through the emptiness inside her stomach, almost doubling her over. She wanted to vomit but used all her will to keep the bile inside.

Deep breaths. Deep breaths. She wasn't sure if it was her or the second voice. Either way, the worse of the pain subsided.

Timing her step, she fell in just behind the merchant as he shouldered the small bag of apples and continued through the market crowd. Someone jostled her as they passed. She resisted the impulse to scream at him, holding tight to her fraying nerves and patience. This was it. If she didn't make this score and get some seraphim, she knew she would just curl up in a ditch and die. The thought made her hand's shake.

She palmed the tiny shiv she kept in her pocket. The merchant slowed as someone called out in greeting. She bumped him, ever so slightly, no more than a normal jostling in the thick crowd. Her shiv flicked out. The weight of a purse filled her hand.

'Hey!' the merchant shouted.

Run!

Ducking her head, she flitted through the crowd. Where the bulky merchant tried to bull his way through, she slid between the people. Where the merchant bashed into people and created more blocks for himself, she used others to break his view of her. Her diminishing size was an advantage here.

Minutes later, she huddled down in a dark alley, all signs of pursuit gone. Her hands shook, this time from anticipation as she drew the strings of the purse open. Something moved in a pile of refuse beside her, but she ignored it. What was one more rat bite when she finally had coin for seraphim?

Tears welled up. She took a shuddering breath.

The purse was filled with small pebbles.

Idiot, her second voice said. *Why do you think it was so easy to get away?*

She shook the purse. A single glint shined up at her. Two silver pennies were nestled in among the pebbles. Her hands shook as she reached inside, not entirely confident that it wasn't her mind playing a trick on her. A tear ran down her grime covered cheeks, leaving a track along her face.

Distro, get to the distro before something goes wrong.

Shaking with excitement, jaw tense with anticipation, she made her way through the maze of side streets and back alleys. The city guards only came down those when they had a reason to. It was safer to move around the city that way; at least they were if you avoided the other desperate cretins that inhabited them. She moved quickly. If she tarried too long the others might have started to notice that she looked excited and wonder why. They might try to take her pennies. She would die before letting that happen.

Eyes followed her through the dim and dirty back roads of Zailhiem. She heard a priest down one street telling people to repent their sins and be saved. Probably wouldn't be much longer 'til he ended up face down in a ditch around here. Although the sun would still be up for a few more hours, it was getting dark in the alleys.

Hurry up! her second voice hissed at her. Shaking hands. Always shaking hands. The pit inside ate at her painfully.

Not long now, she told herself.

The square was one of the older ones in the city, an old willow with drooping limbs shaded most of it. A single figure sat on the stone planter box that circled the tree, hood up despite the warm day. Glancing left and right, she scurried across the cobblestones.

'Told you before, Aliya, I ain't no charity,' the hooded figure said. 'And I ain't interested in your bony ass anymore.'

She shuddered, hands shaking. He had not been gentle. As the memory flushed through her, she was almost thankful that her figure was gone but knew she would not have had to wait so long if she still had it. Hate for herself ran hot for a moment, flushing her cheeks and stopping her shaking hands, but it too was consumed by the maw inside her stomach.

'Got coins,' Aliya mumbled.

'Wassat?'

'I got coins,' she repeated, holding out the silver pennies.

He snatched them from her grasp. She let out a little squeak but stopped herself from stumbling backwards. Her heart pounded. She didn't know if it was fear or anticipation. A moment later, she didn't care.

With a flick of his wrist, the distro spirited the coins into his cloak and produced a single stick of seraphim held between two fingers.

It was almost too much for her. The sight of that single white stick, barely longer than her pinky, brought physical relief. She wanted it. She hated it. She needed it. It would save her life by spiriting her mind away from the hell in which she lived.

Take it, her second voice urged.

Her hand twitched.

'Two pennies should get me more than one,' she said. She fought down the urge to groan at her own words, to hit herself in the face for her stupidity.

The distro paused, then slowly started moving the seraphim away from her. 'Well, if you don't want it.'

'No!' she yelled. Her heart hammered in her chest, breath coming in ragged pants as she clenched her fists to stop the shaking.

His face was almost completely veiled in the dark hood, but still she thought she saw the ghost of a smile in the shadows.

Disgust.

That was what she felt as she saw her shaking hand snake out to snatch the white stick away from him. Disgust at the way she muttered her thanks and scurried back across the cobblestones towards the alley that had brought her here. Disgust at the wretchedness of her life.

Everything will be better once you have the seraphim burning in you.

She wanted to throttle the second voice inside her. To bury it. But she knew it was right.

Two alleys. That's as far as she got. Two alleys away and she could bear the emptiness no longer. The need to feed the maw overrode all else. It didn't matter that she would not be safe once she took the seraphim. Besides, she had nothing to steal, and one more man using her would do her little harm.

She curled up behind a pile of garbage. Placing the seraphim stick in her mouth, she let the shudder pass through her. Her hands were shaking harder than ever. It took all of her will to keep them steady long enough to work her striker, her one possession that was valuable above all other things. Valuable, because without it, there was no way to light the precious seraphim stick in her mouth. A snap and a single curl of smoke rose up before her gaunt, dirty face.

She took a hard pull.

Smoke burned her lungs as she took it in.

Her hands stopped shaking.

Calm returned and the bottomless maw was filled. She knew it was still there, but for now, it could be ignored.

A second lungful and the stick was half gone. A happy haze settled over her.

She grinned. Who cared that she was surrounded by the stinking garbage of human waste.

A third lungful. Not much left. She tried to panic about that but couldn't find the energy to care.

A warm feeling spread around her legs. Had she just wet herself? Who cares?

The final lungful. Her eyes were fluttering. It took so much just to keep them open.

Aliya was in her forest meadow. The sun was warm on her naked skin, breeze blowing her silky black hair back from her face. She rubbed her soft hands over her firm belly, letting them run over her full figure. Why did she ever think she had lost her figure? Surely nothing could ever take her beauty away from her.

She took a step, enjoying the way the soft grass felt between her toes.

This was her paradise. Nothing could compare to this place. This place which only the seraphim could provide to her. This sanctuary of warmth and light and rightness. No one could hurt her here. No one could touch her here. Surely this is what the priests spoke of when they spoke of the All-mother's embrace. Nothing in the world could compare to her forest meadow and how it made her feel.

She had never seen a forest meadow before. Aliya had spent her whole life in Zailhiem. But that didn't matter. Not here.

The tree branches swayed above her as she raised her arms and spun in a circle, reveling in her naked body and the warm safeness that encompassed her. Euphoria washed through her whole existence. The feeling was greater than a thousand orgasms. Not that many of the men she had been with could ever get her to that point. That didn't matter to her though. Not here. Not with the bliss that suffused her.

Snap.

The sound of a breaking branch behind her.

No, her second voice said.

'No,' she whispered.

Her happiness fled faster than a lightning strike. Clouds rolled across the blue sky, taking her warmth and light. She shivered, her nakedness suddenly a threat to her instead of being liberating.

It growled behind her.

Aliya wanted to run, to cry out, to throw herself on the ground and close her eyes. But she knew. She knew she would turn and look at the beast.

That is the only name she gave it.

It waited for her now. At first it had only come once in every ten trips to her forest meadow. Now, it was waiting here for her every time. Her sanctuary had been invaded by the beast, and she knew of no way to expel it.

The beast waited. It snorted behind her.

She turned.

Her eyes were downcast. Its two legs were barely shadows beneath its knees. Her eyes traveled up to the loincloth around its waist. It wore a steel girdle around the top, a demonic skull staring out from where the buckle would be, laughing at her with a grotesque, twisted smile. The beast's stomach was flat and muscled. Its chest was muscled like a barbarian, massive shoulders covered in pauldrons that had three curved spikes sticking up, bulging biceps extending from underneath. And then, the head. The rest of the body was like the statue of gods that could be found in Zailhiem, but not the head. It was a cow's skull, with rotting flesh dangling from jaws that held razor sharp teeth. Two large horns curved downward from its crown. Glowing green eyes pierced her, hatred and anger radiating from them like a physical force.

Aliya screamed.

She had seen the beast many times before, yet still, she screamed.

The beast snorted and stepped towards her.

She turned and ran.

Her legs were weak as she pushed through the forest underbrush. Tree branches seemed to reach out and claw at her naked body, trying to hold her back so the beast could have her. What it wanted, she didn't know. She had no intention of finding out.

Her lungs burned. Rain had broken from the grey clouds above her, sheeting over her and leaving her drenched. The trees were now covered in dark green moss, the branches above adding to the dimness, underbrush closing in around her. It was cold here. Her forest meadow was supposed to be warm.

Why is running so hard? She asked herself. Looking down, her firm and curved body had gone flat, flesh hanging loose. Her pleasantly muscled legs were more akin to kindling than to legs. Glancing at the back of her hands as she ran, she saw the bones and veins standing out against the wane and thin skin there.

She stopped running.

What happened to me?

Sinking to her knees, Aliya no longer cared if the beast caught her. Her forest meadow was gone. All that remained was this dark, dank forest around her, filled with rotting things and death.

The beast snorted behind her. She felt its warm, wet breath on the back of her neck.

Falling forward, she let her forehead splash into the fetid mud beneath her. It stunk like a midden heap. She didn't care. Her forest meadow was gone. She knew it. She knew it would never be hers again. The beast had taken it from her and now there was nothing left to do but to kneel in the mud and succumb. Aliya was weak. It was time to surrender.

Warmth.

There was warmth on her back.

The smell of death was gone, the wetness of the beast's breath no longer on the back of her neck.

Aliya raised herself up to her knees and blinked. There was a warm orange glow all around her. It seemed to be coming from the leaves of the giant redwood tree that loomed before her.

This isn't my forest meadow.

She glanced around but everything outside the ring of light was a black abyss. It was like the maw inside of her, the maw that slowly consumed everything. Looking away from the darkness, she studied the tree. Standing, she staggered towards it. With every step, her wasted body filled out again, until her figure was restored to her. Her beauty, strength, and vitality returned. She marveled at herself.

The scent of roses wafted over her. Roses and wild berries, mixed with the scent of clean, fresh tilled earth.

A figure was at the base of the tree. A woman. She looked like she was a mirror of herself.

'Allmother,' she whispered, although she did not know why.

'Aliya,' the figure whispered back. She knew the mirror of herself had said the word, and yet it was as if the very wind itself had spoken.

She sobbed. Closing her eyes, Aliya sank back to the earth.

Screaming.

Her eyes fluttered slightly.

Someone was screaming nearby, the smell of wood smoke thick in the air.

She wanted to ignore it, to close her eyes and go back to that place. A cough racked through her next breath, smoke overwhelming her. Her eyes flashed open.

Smoke filled the alley she had passed out in. The smell of her own piss coating her legs and the rubbish pile she had slept in was overwhelmed by the black smoke billowing between the buildings. More screaming reached her. It wasn't just a single person screaming. That was normal in the alleys. No, it sounded as if it was the whole city.

Two figures sprinted past her through the alley.

'What's happening?' she called after them.

One stopped and looked back, face pale and eyes wide. 'Darklings,' the boy hissed. His friend grabbed his shoulder, and they were running again.

Darklings aren't real, her second voice tried to tell her. *Just a story to frighten little boys and girls.*

The screaming was getting closer.

Aliya looked down the alley. A dark figure formed in the smoke. It was larger than a human, but she couldn't make out much more. Memory of the beast set her heart pounding.

She turned and ran. She ran through burning streets, ignoring the screams of horror and pain.

She ran as fast and hard as her wasted body could manage.

She ran, even after the city walls were behind her, the orange glow of Zailhiem as it burned lighting her way through the night.

4

Lust

Why did they always have to wear those dresses?

Surely they knew how they looked, how their bodies taunted men. The way the material hugged their bosom, how it curved around their hips, and how their ankles flashed from under the hems as they walked.

'Oh Lord, Almighty Laran, grant me the strength to resist the temptresses that abound in this wicked town.'

His prayer was barely a whisper. Knees aching on the wood genuflectorium, he started the liturgy of repentance once more. The acrid smell of the censure washed over him, burning in the aisle where his altar boy had left it while he prayed. One of the nuns, Olga he thought, was making the rounds through the chapel, extinguishing the candles. At least she wore the shapeless vestments of black. But still, her fair face taunted him with its round shape and smooth skin.

I wonder what colour her hair is under the coif.

The stray thought halted his prayer. With a sigh, he started the liturgy again, clenching his eyes shut tight, ignoring Olga as she passed him in the pews. He certainly didn't breathe deeper. Didn't notice the fresh smell of soap and violet that wafted from her.

Mass today had been a difficult one. Young Margaret Miller had sat in the front row, directly in front of the pulpit. At fifteen summers, she had the figure of a woman but the innocence of an adolescent still. Her long strawberry blonde hair had flowed gracefully down her back; the first time she had not been wearing a child's braid to mass. And her shy smile. That had been the worst, especially as she stepped close to him for the sacrament.

'Grant me the strength, Almighty Laran, to live in your glory and in honour of your tenets,' he continued to pray.

He missed Father Alban desperately. His old mentor would have known what to say to him, would have known how to suppress his unholy urges. The third tenet of Laran was "thou shalt not covet thy neighbour's wife nor daughter". A tear pushed its way from between his clenched eyes, rolling down his freshly shaved cheek.

The rough spun wool of his robe was harsh on his face as he used a corner of his sleeve to wipe away the tear. He opened his eyes and looked up to the image of Laran above the alter, sitting on his golden throne, staring down at him in silent judgement.

A loud thump on the portal made him jump. Sunlight flooded into the chapel as the double door was opened, plunging it into darkness again as the intruder hurriedly closed it behind themselves.

'Mass is over,' he said over his shoulder.

'Please Father,' a delicate voice said, soft footsteps on the stone floor advancing towards him. 'I need help. I need guidance or I fear I will stray from Laran's embrace.'

His breath caught as he turned in surprise.

'Yesmina.'

'Please Father,' she repeated. She crossed her arms, dress pulling tight across her ample chest and looked at her feet. 'Will you help me?'

Why did she have to press her bosom so with her crossed arms. His eyes slid over her raven hair, pulled back with a thin red ribbon that stood out starkly. Her dress was a demure blue, high collared like most in the town, and yet it still showed too much of her womanly curves.

He closed his eyes and took a deep breath. *Is that lavender?* He wondered as her scent reached him.

'Father?' She asked when he remained silent, raising her dark eyes to meet his.

'Of course I will help you, my dear.' Raising a hand, he beckoned her to join him in the pew. 'What troubles you so? I did not see you in mass today.'

Yesmina made the sign of penitence as she stepped into the pew, sitting on the bench next to him.

Why must she so close? He could practically feel her body heat radiating through the scant fabric that separated their flesh. Should he reach out and touch her on the shoulder?

She was clearly upset and surely that would be a comforting gesture.

'I was afraid to come. Afraid everyone would know what has been happening to me.' She sniffed and wiped her nose with a kerchief.

He couldn't help but notice the way her dress pulled against her body as she reached into her pocket for it.

'What's been happening?' He clenched his eyes shut for a moment and tried to refocus his mind. *Laran give me strength.*

She took a shuddering breath followed by a deeper one. 'I have been having dreams.'

'We all have dreams,' he reassured her. His own dreams flashed to the forefront of his mind. His dream of Yesmina and her raven hair stuck in his mind's eye.

'These are not normal dreams,' she explained. Her delicate white hands were in her lap, clenching the kerchief like it was her only buoy in a tumultuous sea. 'They are dark. Horrible things happen that I swear feel real.'

'Dark dreams are not strange. Again, we all have them.' He wanted her to leave. He needed her to leave. Being this close to her, feeling her next to him on the hard bench, aspect of Laran staring down at him in judgement; it was too much. 'Come to the next mass and pray with the congregation.'

'No! You don't understand.'

Yesmina shifted to face him, dark eyes turning on him and threatening to drown him. The way her hair framed her face, her moist lips, the curve of her neck as it went down into her bodice.

'They aren't just dreams,' she continued in a rush. 'I think … I think I'm seeing the future.'

He wanted to laugh but the earnest look on her face stopped him.

'Only mighty Laran knows the future,' he said dutifully. 'Only He knows the fate he has laid out for all of us.'

Tears streamed freely down Yesmina's pale cheeks. Even in the dim light within the chapel, they were clear. 'I know,' she sobbed. 'But I also know that what I am seeing is real. They are coming and I'm too afraid to tell anyone.'

Her trembling lip taunted him. *What would it feel like to press my lips to hers?* It took a moment for him to realise what she had said.

'Who is coming?' he asked.

'Darklings,' she whispered.

He blinked. 'What did you say?'

'Darklings.'

He huffed a small laugh. 'Darklings are nothing but pagan fables.'

She shook her head. Clearly she was delusional. But still, her skin was so soft, her lips so lush. *Perhaps I could just …* Reaching across, he brushed a stray hair off her cheek.

'They are real,' she said quietly but firmly.

He rested his hand on her shoulder and slid closer. *Definitely lavender.* Sliding his arms across her shoulders, he leaned in.

'What are you doing?' She tried to pull away from him, but he held her firm against his body.

What am I doing? The thought flashed through his mind and yet he could not find the strength of will to stop himself. Her body was pressed tight against him now.

She tried to push him off, but his young arms were still strong despite the sedentary life of priesthood.

'It's fine, it's fine,' he muttered to her.

Kicking and pushing, she squealed, trying to get him off her. Her squirming only enflamed him more. Her soft lips tasted like honey even if she was clenching them shut against him, twisting her head back and forth to get away from him.

'No, Father, no!'

I'm sorry Almighty Laran. He reached down with one hand, grabbing a handful of her dress and yanking it up, his other hand fending off her feeble attempts to stop him. *Surely if I wasn't meant to do this, He would stop me.*

'No!' Yesmina screamed.

Too late he saw that she had been reaching towards the aisle. An altar boy had left a censure burning beside him as he prayed, its smoke had not been enough to drown out the feminine smell. She gripped it and swung; a snarl plastered across her face.

Pain blossomed in his head. He felt it knock against something as he fell off Yesmina. His vision blurred. Yesmina stood above him, looking down at where he lay, panting as she pushed her dress down with one hand, censure in the other. She saw him watching her. She swung the censure again.

All was darkness.

He couldn't see. He couldn't hear. But he was aware.

Mighty Laran, what did I do?

Deep in the black abyss, his heart broke. He wasn't sure if he had tears, wherever he was, but he let them flow freely in his mind.

'Micah.'

He heard the voice call his name. It was a voice and yet he wasn't sure where it came from. Almost it was as if the wind carried it to him.

A light.

There was a light in the distance. He moved towards it. Surely it was the light of Laran, that he had found his way to His eternal embrace.

At one moment the light was in the distance and the next he was bathed in a warm orange glow. He expected to see the aspect of Laran on his golden throne. Instead, a giant redwood tree rose before him. Staring up in awe, he realised the orange glow was coming from the leaves of the tree.

'What is this heresy?' he whispered.

'Micah,' the bodiless voice called again.

He walked towards the trunk of the redwood. Everything outside the orange light it was emitting was an abyss of darkness.

'Micah.'

A figure stood at the trunk of the tree, almost as if rising from the too green grass that surrounded it. He couldn't seem to focus on it. Its figure was feminine in a way he had never imagined before, and yet he felt no desire. There were no features to the ephemeral woman. She just was.

'Micah.'

'Allmother,' he whispered back.

His eyes closed as the tears came. *It has all been a lie.* His guilt hit him even harder. The knowledge of what he had tried to do, what he had almost done, tore him apart. He wanted it all to end.

'Don't let me wake,' he said to the Allmother. 'Let me fall into the black abyss.'

He couldn't see her, but somehow he knew that she smiled at him.

The smell of smoke was the first sensation that came back to him. His head pounded. Reaching up, his hand came away bloody. Blinking his eyes, his vision slowly focused. He was still laying in the pew of his chapel where Yesmina had hit him.

Fire licked across the roof and the walls. Smoke billowed everywhere. He coughed as he looked around at what had so recently been his sanctuary. Breathing became difficult. The doors were standing open, and he took off in a hunched sprint towards them. He took a deep breath as he stepped out into the courtyard, which sent him into a coughing fit.

As the fit subsided he looked up. *Where are the townsfolk? Why aren't they fighting the fire?*

A scream rent the air, sending his blood cold.

Bodies. The figures around the small courtyard were his nuns. The three women had been torn to shreds, red blood pooling around them on the stones. His chapel was not the only building on fire. It looked as if half the town was burning.

A groan drew his attention.

'Olga,' he gasped. Running over, he kneeled at her side, taking her hand in his, ignoring the blood. 'What happened?'

She gasped and blood gushed from her mouth. 'Darklings,' she mumbled through the blood.

Her hand went lax in his own as his mind tried to understand what she had said. 'Darklings are just fables,' he whispered to himself.

Noticing she had passed; he placed her hand gently on her chest and closed her eyes. He thought about administering last rites but now he knew how futile that was. The smell finally washed over him.

He turned and vomited.

More screams from the town.

He stood. His legs shook and he almost collapsed. Something was moving towards him.

Allmother protect me, he prayed silently.

Micah ran.

5

Vengeance

A black raven cawed from the twisted tree branch above her, seeming to mock her as she pushed through the branches. The old path was overgrown in places, making her trek more difficult than it had to be, and yet she pushed onwards. She let out a yawn.

'That trader better have been right,' she muttered to herself.

Taking a moment, she looked around, trying to decide on a good place to camp for the night. The shadows in the forest were lengthening. Sickly, gnarled trees surrounded her, casting shadows that looked like the limbs of demons reaching out to grab her. She shivered. The evening was warm under the canopy. Still, a cold crept inside her. There was something tainted about this forest, something wrong and which defied definition. It was not a pretty forest, not like the groves around the College, but to the naked eye there appeared to be nothing wrong with it. Trees and grass grew, small animals skittered along the ground and through the tree branches, birds such as that annoying raven flapped and cawed. But Rinalta could feel it. Something was resonating with her Centre, disrupting her mana flow ever so slightly.

The telltale snap of a branch brought her attention back to the present. The noise had echoed back to her from further along the beaten path. Hunching down, Rinalta eased her way forward, careful not to brush the branches that were reaching out towards her. She stepped slowly in the fading light, body tense, a bead of sweat rolling down the side of her face.

A shadow burst from the scrub ahead of her, sprinting along the path.

It's him!

She took off after him, heedless now of the branches or noise she was making. Her quarry had never been so close, and the rage flamed hot inside her at the sight of him. Heart pounding, Rinalta cursed as a tree branch whipped across her face. Wiping away what she thought must be blood on her cheek, she looked up and pulled herself to a stop. The shadow had disappeared. The darkness of night was closing in around her, made all the deeper by the canopy above her.

Idiot, she cursed herself softly. Of course there was no way she could have kept up with him. It would have been so simple to cast an entangling spell on his legs, trip him up and give her time to pull on her mana reserves to conjure a set of mystical bindings. Rinalta let out a sigh. *What would Mas-*

ter Gerard think of this poor display? He had always told her to slow down, to think before she acted.

There was a pale light coming from further up the path. It looked like a break in the trees where the last rays of sunlight were still managing to creep in, or at very least some early moonlight. She sighed and started trudging up the path again, hoping to find a meadow where she could sleep under the stars instead of under gnarled tree branches. There was also the feint hope that her quarry might have the same thought. She wiped her sweaty palms on her pants and reached up to check her cheek again. It was raw and painful, but she didn't feel blood anymore, so she tried not to worry too much. The urge to reach into her Centre and use some mana to heal it was there of course, but healing something you couldn't see was risky. Better to wait until she could pull her tiny travel mirror out of her pack. She wasn't particularly vain, and yet she also had no desire to have a scratch marring her face if she could help it.

Pulling herself from her musings, Rinalta looked up the path again. *Keep your mind on what you're doing,* she said to herself, repeating a line her master had constantly repeated to her. Her steps faltered as a building came into view, lit by the moonlight coming through a break in the canopy.

A flock of bats burst from the tree above her, fluttering around her head. She shrieked and ducked down, hands waving to ward them off as the cloud of flying rodents fluttered off towards the house.

Rinalta took a breath to calm herself, definitely not thinking about how the bats had touched her. She rubbed her hands together as if she could wipe away the feeling. Hoping they weren't finding a way into the house, she started up the path again. It was an old manor house, three stories tall with a sloped tile roof and brick chimney poking out the top. The wood walls had been weathered to grey, water damage obvious as she approached, but it seemed sturdy enough to her untrained architectural eye.

'Creepy,' she muttered to herself, eyeing the glass windows that were so covered in grime that she couldn't see through them. Rinalta considered sleeping outside but couldn't resist having a roof over her head again, even if it wasn't the best maintained roof. She sighed as she thought of her room at the College of Rel. At the time it had seemed small and cramped. Now she would give anything to be there again, comfortable and warm and clean and with her master.

Shaking the thoughts from her head, she approached the weather-beaten double door, ignoring the way the stairs to the veranda creaked and sagged as they took her weight. The veranda was empty of all except dead leaves that had blown in and got stuck, the corner of the roof drooping ever so slightly. There was a wood rail around the veranda however from the look of it, Rinalta didn't think it would even hold her own slight weight if she leaned against it. Stepping up to the door, she gently turned the metal doorknob. It squeaked softly in protest but turned easily enough. Giving it a push, the door swung inwards, screeching horribly on rusted hinges, the sound echoing through the house. Rinalta winced as she looked inside.

So much for being stealthy, she thought to herself.

The only light inside was the moonlight coming through the grime-covered windows, leaving most of the interior in darkness. Rinalta waited a moment, peering into the dark, straining her eyes to see if she could detect any movement before thinking to cast a detect life spell. Summoning her mana, she focused its energy into the correct configuration for the spell and released it, feeling the power flow out from her and into the building. To her surprise, she felt not one, but two people in the old house, although they were in separate areas. There were plenty of smaller life forms in the house, likely rats or bats - she shivered at the thought. Letting the threads of power return to her Centre, she reached in again and channeled mana to her left hand, configuring it into a small ball of pale blue light. Its soft glow illuminated the entry hall as she stepped over the threshold. A small part of her chided herself for never mastering internal configuration spells like the night eyes spell, but there was little she could do about it now.

A sliding door to her right was ajar, showing an empty sitting room, its moth-eaten furniture just lumps in the dark. She ignored it. The two life forms she detected were on the second floor. There was no wall to her left, the entrance hall opening into an atrium with large windows that struggled to allow the moonlight to enter through the grime and leaves coating it. Couches and divans were spread haphazardly through the atrium, the once fine fabric that coated them turned to mould and dust, and likely one small push away from total collapse.

She walked slowly past the atrium and through a portal at the end of the hall. Large doors led left and right, the master staircase in front of her leading her up. She could see a small door under the stairs, likely for servants or a door to a basement. There was no way she was going to find out.

Groaning ominously under her weight, Rinalta took a deep breath and started up the stairs. With every step she expected them to give way and send her plummeting down into who knows what. They held. Rinalta rolled her shoulders, trying to loosen the tension there, letting the straps of her pack settle as she looked first left and then right down the hallway. It was lined with doors which likely led to bedrooms or sitting rooms. There were paintings along the walls, one between almost every door, sometimes two. Time had not been kind to them. The paint was chipped and faded until the subjects were just blurry blobs, whatever they had once depicted now lost to time. She could see a recess at the end of the hallway to her right where a set of stairs led up to the third floor. Not particularly wanting to face another set of rickety stairs just then, she opted to go left first. If her life sense spell had been accurate, one of the life forms was in the room at the end of the hallway.

She let the power to her ball of light recede, the glow dimming itself in response. Reaching into her Centre, she bundled up her mana, holding it ready in case she had to defend herself. Master Gerard had always been disappointed in her ability to direct her mana internally, but external spells, particularly the destructive kind, came naturally to her. Almost too naturally her master had once said.

The floorboards beneath her feet creaked ominously. She banished thoughts of falling through the floor from her mind. An echo, the lingering effect of the life sense spell, told her the lifeform was in the last door on the right. A sense of euphoria washed through her. It was the familiar feeling of power that came from wielding her mana. And that power would give her vengeance.

Sending a trickle of mana through her body and into her legs, she kicked the loose-fitting door right off its hinges. Rushing into the room, heart pounding, she let her small bulb of blue light morph into a raging orange ball of fire. It bathed the room in light. Rinalta fed all her hatred and rage into the flame, creating a small point of concentrated fury, ready to throw at the deceiver and wreak her vengeance upon him. Cocking her arm, she readied herself to throw it in his lying, murderous, vile face.

The rage in her hand died.

Huddled in the far corner, trying to escape the light, was a person. It took a moment for Rinalta to realise it was a woman, she was so malnourished and skinny, collar bones sticking out sickly, her tattered dress barely staying on her frame.

The ball of fire in her hand sputtered out as she released her mana, absently noting it rush back into her Centre. It was a pleasurable feeling, but one that could easily be ignored once you were used to it. Keeping a trickle still contained in her hand, Rinalta morphed the orange flame back into the blue orb of light and leaned in, trying to get a closer look at the woman.

'I'm not going to hurt you,' Rinalta said, hunching over, trying to get a better look at her face.

The woman tried to scuttle back again. She was a pitiful creature; all knobby bones covered in a layer of grime and dirt. One of the woman's sleeves had been torn free and the hem of the dress was tattered and fraying, well above the ankles and likely threading higher every day. The woman looked up at Rinalta with hollow, black rimmed eyes that were sunken back into her skull. Rinalta saw a burn mark on her lips.

Seraphim user, Rinalta thought to herself. *That explains the state she's in.*

'What's your name?' Rinalta asked the addict, trying to keep her voice soft and calm.

The addict flinched but looked up at her again. 'Aliya,' she whispered with a hoarse voice.

'I'm looking for a man. Have you seen anyone else in this house?'

Aliya shook her head too quickly.

'I can protect you,' she said, holding her hand out.

'I ...'

'Yes?'

'I saw a man come in not long ago. I hid in here.' Aliya reached out and put her hand in Rinalta's.

She helped the addict to her feet, wondering how the woman had the strength to stand on those bony sticks called legs. Even the woman's hand felt frail, like that of a wizened old lady, not a young woman that should be in her prime. 'Do you know where the man went? What he looked like?' The woman just shook her head.

'I need to go find him. You stay here and –'

'No!' She clasped Rinalta's hand in a vice like grip. 'Don't leave me here alone.'

Rinalta thought about pointing out that she had been here alone until just a moment ago but decided against it. She doubted it would change her mind; the woman had a death grip on Rinalta's hand. 'Alright. Stay behind me and stay quiet.' She shook Aliya's hand off her saying, 'I'll need both hands.'

Aliya puffed in ragged breaths as they started down the hallway. Rinalta wondered if her breathing came from damaged lungs from the seraphim, from her emaciated state, or simply fear.

The lingering echo of her life sense was well and truly gone now. Her last lingering feeling had put the other life form in a room at the other end of the hall. She didn't bother casting the spell again. She could recast if he had managed to avoid her. After months chasing the murderer, Rinalta knew speed was of the essence.

A gasp made her spin. Aliya had one hand outstretched, leaning against the wall. 'Dizzy,' she explained.

Putting a finger to her lips, she tried not to regret helping the woman. Rinalta purposely didn't think what she would do if Aliya refused to leave after she finished here. Waving her on behind her, she continued down the hall.

A loud racking cough pulled them to a halt again, her blue orb extinguishing in an instant. It came from a partially open door just ahead. From what she could see, the door wouldn't close because of the warped door frame. Rinalta waited. No more sounds reached her. Pressing herself against the wall, glancing back to make sure Aliya did the same, she started inching forward, ignoring the pounding of her own heart that she was sure would give her away. Her new ward had looked ashen behind her. Leaning forward slightly, she tried to peer through the small gap in the door.

The unmistakable rasp of steel leaving a leather sheathe came from the room.

'I know you're there,' a harsh, guttural voice called from the room. 'Enter slowly or I'll gut you like a pig.'

Her heart thudded in her chest. *When had his voice become so rough? And since when did he use a sword?* Aliya pawed at her arm as she stepped forward to open the door. A bead of sweat rolled down her cheek.

Rinalta pushed the door open, wincing as its hinges squealed. She stood in the door frame and looked at the rough man across the room, holding a short sword out in front of him.

'You're not Claudius,' she said.

A clap of thunder sounded, rattling the windows in their frames.

Her vengeance had been snatched from her once again. Her heart dropped.

6

Vengeance

'Who the fuck is Claudius?' the grizzled man said.

He didn't lower his sword, its point not wavering an inch as he glared at Rinalta across the dust-strewn room. She couldn't help but sniff as the dust went up her nose. The sniff quickly triggered her and she sneezed, the blue orb in her hand wavering as her concentration slipped and the configuration for the spell wavered. Feeling any sense of menace she may have possessed fleeing as she wiped her nose on her sleeve, she straightened.

'Who are you?' she asked.

'Who am I? Who the fuck are you? You were the one trying to sneak up and attack me. And who the fuck is Claudius?' A floorboard in the corridor creaked. 'Tell whoever is out there to come in, slowly. One false move and I'll gut you.'

'Alright,' Rinalta said, holding up both hands. The blue orb stuck to her hand as she did so, and she suppressed a smirk as the grizzled man's eye's glanced at it. He was built like a soldier with broad shoulders and thick sausage fingers that were more comfortable grasping a sword than a hoe or pickaxe. She had been forced to study hand-to-hand combat at the College of Rel, one of the more unsavory aspects of her tuition. Her skill had been adequate at best, but she knew enough to notice that he favoured his right leg. *An old injury?* she wondered, looking for any advantage if the situation came to blows. His hair was thinning, a dark shade of brown from what she could tell in the dim room.

'Now!' he hissed, poking the sword tip towards the door.

'Aliya, please come in and join us.'

Rinalta heard a whimper from behind her before the floor squeaked again. The addict shuffled in, head bowed low and bony fingers clasping at the skirt of her dress.

'As you can see," Rinalta said in a soothing voice. Or, at least, as soothing as she could get. She always envied the way Stablemaster Trell had been able to calm animals and people, with his voice alone. Her own voice, she had been told by multiple people, was far too imperious to achieve it. 'This woman is no threat to you, so might I suggest that we all calm ourselves and start with introductions.'

The soldier's eyes flicked back and forth between them, weighing her words. He assented with a curt nod, the sword tip lowering to the floorboards, although Rinalta couldn't help but note that he didn't move to put it away.

'Very well,' Rinalta said. She let out a pent-up breath. With her free hand, she pushed a lock of her raven hair back behind her ear and tried to ignore Aliya's feeble attempt to grab at her arm. 'My name is Rinalta, and this is Aliya, whom I just met here in this house.' She waited. 'And you are?' she prompted when the soldier was not forthcoming.

He chewed his lip before answering. 'Name's Oswald. Legionary of the Order of Light.'

'Well Oswald, it's a pleasure to make your acquaintance.'

He snorted. 'Give it time.' Groaning, he lowered himself to sit on a small trunk that she hadn't noticed was behind him, its lid sagging under his weight. He was certainly favouring his right leg. 'Now, gunna tell me who the fuck Claudius is?' He placed the sword across his knees and waved his hand at the floor, inviting them to sit.

'He is a murderer I have been chasing,' Rinalta said. She saw little reason to withhold the truth from this man. He was clearly in pain and likely on the run himself. She thought she saw his eye twitch, but it was hard to tell in the dark.

'All men are murderers,' he muttered. Rinalta didn't think the remark was meant as a reply to her statement, although it was hard to tell. She'd never been great at reading people. He was flexing his hand open and closed.

A crack of thunder came from outside, the sound of approaching rain and wind blowing through the gnarled limbs of the trees making a ruckus. Aliya gave a short scream, huddling her knees up to her chin.

'Well,' Rinalta said, ignoring his words and the addict's outburst of fear, 'I have tracked him for near two moons now and thought I had caught him as darkness fell. I assumed he sought refuge in this building but apparently it was just one of you two.' Rinalta placed the blue orb on the floor between them, siphoning a touch more mana into it to brighten the room.

'It wasn't me, I've been here for over a day,' Oswald said, squinting at Aliya across the blue orb.

The addict shook her head as Rinalta turned to look at her. 'Don't know how long I've been here, couple of hours I guess.'

It was him, she thought to herself. The thought gave her hope but also a sense of futility; to have been so close to him and still fail weighed on her. Surely Master Gerard would have caught him by now and returned to the College of Rel an even greater hero than he already was.

Another crack of thunder and lightning preceded a gale of rain hitting the grimy, near black window.

'And what brought you here, Oswald?' she asked, if only to break her morose train of thought. It occurred to her that she never asked Aliya that question either, and that she had no idea where the seraphim addict had come from or why she was in a dilapidated house in the middle of the woods. Surely, there was no seraphim here.

His eye twitched again and he shifted, stifling a groan and glaring at her. 'What's it to you?'

'Just being polite and trying to get to know you. From the sound of that storm, it will be around most of the night, so we should probably get comfortable here with each other.'

'Hmm. Guess so.'

Rinalta suppressed a sigh. She hated having to draw things out of people. Why couldn't they just tell her what she wanted to know and do what she wanted? Things would be so much simpler. She was obviously intelligent and had more schooling than most, so why didn't they just listen to her and do what she wanted?

So?" she prodded, arching an eyebrow at him. The storm reached them. In an instant, the constant patter of rain on the roof and window filled the room with a backdrop of noise.

'Fine,' he growled, stretching his left leg out before him with a grimace and placing his sword on the floor beside him. 'If you must know, I'm trying to get to Yamir.'

'That's a hike,' Rinalta commented. Oswald just grunted. 'Are you coming from the outpost near Reshi?' It was a stab in the dark, an educated guess based on what she knew about the area, but the way his eyes glazed over told her she had found a mark.

'The outpost ain't there anymore.' His fists clenched, scarred knuckles turning white.

'Not there? What do you... how?'

'Darklings.' Oswald's answer was barely a whisper. Aliya squeaked as a peel of thunder shook the glass in the window frame.

Rinalta couldn't help the laugh that escaped her. 'You seriously expect me to believe that a fairy tale destroyed –'

'They're no fairy tale!' Oswald was breathing hard like he had just run a race, the hand massaging his left knee had a not-so-subtle tremor. 'They overran the outpost in the middle of the night. We tried to fight back but they... they... we couldn't stop them.' Tears welled in his eyes.

'They're real,' Aliya whispered into the silence. Rinalta closed her mouth and looked across at the emaciated woman, her shaking taking on a new light. 'I'm from Zailheim.'

'I was in Zailheim only two weeks ago,' Rinalta said, her hushed tone matching Aliya's.

'It's now just a graveyard.' There was loss in her voice but also something else, something akin to her own thirst for vengeance.

Rain battered against the window. The blue light of her orb cast a too constant glow over all of them. She absently wished they had a fire, the warm orange glow was always far more soothing than light orbs, and the warmth would be welcome. A cold had washed over Rinalta, a cold that she didn't think came from the draught that blew through the old manor.

'But... Darklings... I mean –'

'I already fucking told you, they're real.' Oswald reached for his sword, almost unconsciously.

'How can they be real? I mean, this is just...'

'It's the end of the world,' Aliya whispered when she trailed off.

Both Oswald and Rinalta stared at her.

'That's why you're going to Yamir?' she asked Oswald, if only to break the tension.

He nodded. 'The Order needs to know. We need to prepare a defence, find a way to stop them.'

'You're a soldier? A legionary?' Aliya asked him.

Oswald snorted; lips curled. He glanced at Aliya and his expression softened. 'Yes,' he answered. 'I was put out to pasture at the Reshi outpost, too many injuries.' He flexed his leg and then groaned, clutching at his side.

'You're still injured,' Aliya gasped, covering her mouth with a hand.

Rinalta saw a wet patch seeping through his shirt. 'That looks bad,' she said.

'You're bleeding,' Aliya added uselessly.

'Had worse.'

'I could help. I'm a mage.'

The silence stretched.

'You're going to feint soon,' Aliya said. 'I've seen it before, when someone loses too much blood.'

Oswald considered the addict, taking in her frail frame and tattered dress before nodding his assent to Rinalta. He tried to pull his shirt over his head, groaning and stopping with it half-way up his body and near collapsing onto his side. Aliya rushed forward and caught him before Rinalta could. She was amazed the woman had the strength to hold the burly soldier upright.

'Stop trying to help,' Rinalta snapped at him as he pawed at his shirt again. 'Hold him steady, Aliya, while I get his shirt.'

Together, they manage to get his shirt off. Aliya held him upright with one arm while Rinalta unwound the dirty bandage from around his chest. He had a nasty gash that ran from his left pectoral down his side almost to his buttock. Oswald was swaying slightly, fluttering eyes half-closed as he tried to remain conscious. She inspected the wound, moving his arm out of the way as she moved around him, stopping behind him as she saw the scars. It took all her will not to gasp. Apart from all the myriad of small scars one would expect to find on a professional soldier's body, three giant gashes ran down the length of his back. *Like claw marks,* she thought to herself. But there was no way he could have been clawed by darklings and been healed by now, not going off the loose timeline he had provided and the distance from the Reshi outpost.

'That's a nasty scratch.' Even she wasn't sure if she meant the wound she was tending or the claw scars. Oswald's only response was a grunt.

Ignoring his sharp intakes of breath and low growls, Rinalta poked at the wound, inspecting where the flesh was torn, seeing what muscles needed to be reknitted together under the skin. Healing was delicate work. Not exactly her strong suit. But still, the wound was simple as far as the human body went and she could heal it with minimal complication. Reaching into her Centre, she pulled forth a large amount of mana and started weaving it into a complex configuration, ensuring she placed each weave perfectly. The power built as she set the configuration. Warmth seeped out through her hand as she pushed the mana into Oswald, watching as his flesh knit itself back together. Once the process was complete, she prodded at the smooth skin where the wound had been only moments before. As far as she could tell, the muscle had knitted back together properly; hopefully there wouldn't be any complications. That could happen sometimes, and if it did, there would be little more she could do to remedy it.

'That works better than a bottle of rum,' Oswald said, eyes now open and alert as he looked down at his own body.

'Lift your arm for me,' Rinalta ordered. He did as he was told, working his arm up and down then rolling it in its socket. 'It looks like the muscle has healed properly, although it's hard to tell for sure.' Aliya was still holding him by his other side. 'You can let him go now.'

She thought she saw the addict blush as she released him and rejoined Rinalta on the floor.

'I... Uh, thank you,' Oswald said. His hesitant voice had softened; he was clearly unused to giving honest thanks.

Rinalta nodded and fought off the wave of fatigue that came crashing down on her. Healing magic always took a lot of mana, enough to exhaust even experienced mages, a category which did not include her. She blew out a sigh and rubbed the back of her neck, closing her eyes and focusing on her Centre, taking stock of her mana reserve.

'What do we do now?' Aliya asked in a quiet voice.

'Rest,' Rinalta said.

'Aye,' Oswald agreed. The old soldier looked as tired as Rinalta felt.

Although now that he wasn't losing blood and half dead, Rinalta realised that he wasn't as old as she had first thought.

Perhaps in his late thirties. The scars, scowl, and aura of a warrior had aged him.

A gust of wind blew rain hard against the window, shaking it in its frame once again. Rinalta lay on the floor, using her pack as a pillow.

'Here,' Oswald said gruffly, handing Aliya a tattered cloak that was likely once a dark blue, but now it was grey.

'Thank you.'

She actually looks shy, Rinalta thought to herself, eyes fluttering open and shut. Exhaustion was overtaking her, but still, she felt shame that she hadn't thought to share her own cloak. Aliya's dress was barely more than rags, and she had no meat on her bones, something common after years of seraphim use - she must have been freezing. *I'll share some food with them in the morning,* Rinalta consoled herself. She let the blue orb fade, reclaiming what little mana was left in it back into her Centre.

A loud bang echoed through the house, jerking Rinalta from her half-asleep state.

'What was that?' Aliya squeaked, clutching the cloak to her chest.

Another bang. A door being slammed shut.

'Claudius,' Rinalta hissed. Scrambling to her feet, she reached into her diminished Centre, rushing for the door.

'Wait!' Oswald hissed.

It was too late. She was through the ill-fitting door an instant later, configuration for a fireball building in her hand.

Rinalta would have her vengeance.

7

Lust

Rain sheeted down from the sky in waves, battering him from every side as the wind whipped about. His finger joints felt locked together from the cold. Every attempt to move them resulted in pain, a jolting pain unlike any he had felt before.

This is my punishment, Micah thought to himself. *This is the hell that was promised by Laran.*

Surely, if the Allmother was real, if that pagan god really did sit under her glowing tree of life, then surely, surely, the Almighty Laran is real as well. Or at least, that is what he had been trying to convince himself. Everything that had happened since the darklings overran his chapel and destroyed the flea-bitten town that he had tended to was surely a test of his piety, a test from the one true god to ensure he was worthy.

'Yes, that's definitely it,' he said out loud to himself. Not that he could hear himself over the storm, and his voice definitely didn't crack with a note of hysteria.

He stumbled in the dark, foot catching on something hard, sending him tumbling forward into the cold, wet mud. His once immaculate brown robe was already soaked through. And yet, he still winced more at the water that seeped through to touch his skin than at the pain that jolted through his knees and wrists as they took the brunt of the impact. It was cold and a little slimy against his skin. Micah shuddered. It was just rain on his face, definitely not tears.

Venturing into the woods had seemed like such a sensible thing to do as he had fled the darklings. He had enjoyed walking through the woods around Yamir during his time as an acolyte at the temple. The paths had been a pleasant reprieve from days indoor at his studies and prayer. Other acolytes had preferred to explore the city and all the wonders the capital of a prosperous empire could offer, but for Micah, there had been far too much temptation; far too many beautiful women. An hour or two walking the paths, stopping at the streams to cool his feet, or simply to lay in the grass strewn meadows had been far more relaxing. How he missed Yamir and its comforts. This wood had proven far different, far more wild and uncouth, more unforgiving than that of his youth.

Micah sat in the mud, unable to summon the will to stand and keep moving. He could barely see for the darkness, the flash of lightning proving more hinderance than help as it destroyed what little night vision he had with every crack.

'Help me Almighty Laran,' he sobbed.

There was no response. There was never a response. For years he had begged for help from his deity, to help rid him of the immoral thoughts and desires that had plagued him since his foundling years. Micah hung his head and let the tears flow, his sobbing and wailing thrown to and lost on the wind as the storm raged around him, body shaking with cold and despair alike.

I should just curl up here in the mud and let the storm consume me, he thought, letting the maw of despair in his chest open up. *At least I haven't had a lustful thought in days.* He couldn't help the chuckle that rose in him at the thought.

Raising his head, Micah saw an orange glow in the distance.

'Allmother?'

His first thought had been of the glowing orange tree, the place he had been transported to after giving way to his evil, lustful urges, when he had tried to force himself on Yesmina. Shame flushed through him, almost strong enough to warm his frozen bones. Had he returned to that place? Had the storm finally consumed his frail body, leaving his soul for the Allmother to claim in place of his rightful deity?

Wiping his face, he blinked water from his eyes. The gnarled branches of trees outlined themselves before the small orange glow, giving him a sense of distance in the dark. *That's a fire!* Hope thrummed through him, and he forced his aching cold body to move once again, ignoring the slimy feeling of water and mud that had invaded inside his robe. Groping in the dark, he made his way forward, blinking rain from his eyes and grasping branches to help keep himself upright. Any pride he might have felt at being an outdoorsman was shattered. He fell several times, panic hitting him like a wave every time he fell; panic that the orange glow of light would disappear in the storm and he would once again be cold and alone. Stepping up onto a root in his path, he could finally make out a small shack, barely a lean-to really, with a tiny campfire nestled at the back, the figure of a person sitting before it with their back to the storm. A small walk down a hill and he would have warmth, shelter, and company. He refused to believe that this person, no matter how callous, would deny him a spot in his shelter or to share the warmth of the fire.

Micah went to take a step off the root, to start down the small hill that separated himself from warmth, when his foot slipped on the rain slicked, moss covered wood.

The world tumbled. Or rather, he tumbled. Darkness spun around him, the flicker of flame occasionally breaking it, pain shooting through his body faster than he could register. Over and over in a never-ending loop of pain and disorientation.

It stopped as suddenly as it had begun. One moment Micah was spinning, limbs a chaotic jumble as he tumbled, then with a crunch that drove the breath from his lungs the world was once again still. It was the rain pooling in his eyes that forced him to move first. Just a slight tilt of his head as he sucked air as hard as he could, lungs refusing to inflate properly, a wheezing noise eking from him. He whimpered. Where was he? What was he doing again? Rolling to his side took more effort than anything he could remember but he was rewarded, for a brief glimpse at least, by the sight of the glow of warm firelight.

Then a dark figure stepped between him and the promise of sanctuary.

'Fucking hell that was one hell of an entrance,' a high voice said, loud over the ever-present noise of the storm. 'What the hell were you thinking, running down a hill in the middle of a storm? I'm amazed you didn't brain yourself on a rock or break your neck.' The man talked in a constant stream, like every thought he had spilled from him in a torrent he couldn't control. Micah didn't care. The man was helping him up, taking his weight which he was grateful for as his traitorous legs wobbled under him. His knees threatened to buckle with every hobbling step, the effort taking what little air his struggling lungs were able to suck in. 'That's it buddy, just a few more steps. Watch your head here, gotta duck under the roof. It ain't the strongest roof and I don't wanna risk wrecking the only shelter out here.'

The man helped him crawl under the lean-to, the small fire warming him despite its pitiful size and way it spluttered as the wind blew.

'Thank you,' Micah managed to wheeze.

The man waved it away and settled himself next to him by the little fire, feeding it with a small bundle of sticks. 'What's so important to have you out in a storm like this, especially this deep in the woods?' The man's constant litany finally stopped as he waited for an answer.

Micah stared at him for a moment, wondering how to answer. The man was slim, but not skinny. More athletic than anything, with long graceful limbs that were well muscled but not bulky. Like a dancer, Micah thought. His hair was plastered to his head from the rain, hanging lank just below his pointed chin. The man pulled his wet cloak around him and looked back at Micah.

Clearing his throat, he answered, 'I was seeking shelter.'

The man let out a short barking laugh, making Micah jump. 'No shit. But why are you here in the first place?'

'I was... running.' Micah stared into the fire, images of blood and bodies flashing through his mind, heart pounding from the memory.

'Trouble with a woman?'

'Yes,' Micah said. 'What? No!' He shook his head, ignoring the guilt that sat in his chest. 'No, nothing like that. I was... I am a priest of Laran. The village I tended was attacked, everyone was killed, but I managed to escape into the woods. I've been trying to find my way out ever since.'

'Attacked? By who?' The man's grey eyes studied him, orange firelight flickering in them. 'Didn't think we were at war with anyone.'

'It wasn't people.'

'Huh?'

'It was darklings. Or at least, I think it was darklings, that's what Olga said with her dying words. I don't know... I... Uh.' Micah stared at the fire. Now that he had said it out loud to another person, he realised how insane it sounded, and that he had never actually seen what had attacked the village. Only the bloody aftermath. Surely, no man could have created carnage such as he had seen.

The man was staring at him. A shiver ran down his spine at the gaze, a creeping dread worming its way into him. 'What did you say your name was again?' Micah asked him.

Teeth flashed in a quick smile that didn't reach the man's eyes. A crack of thunder lit the woods around their shelter, making Micah jump again. 'Bit jumpy there, Micah.'

'Yes, a little,' he said with a half-hearted chuckle. 'It's been a stressful couple of days. I guess I am a bit on edge. And I... I... wait, how do you know my name?'

Another smile.

Micah started to shake. His heart stopped in his chest as if encased in ice.

'That's not particularly important,' the man said, smile sliding off his face, replaced by a stoney blank slate. 'What's important is that you were not supposed to escape. Darklings are ferocious killers, but not particularly dependable when it comes to details.' He held out a hand as he spoke, a small ball of molten flame appearing in his palm.

A mage, a part of his mind realised in disgust, a part that was detached from the fear.

'Don't worry, I am getting very good at this. It will only hurt for a moment.'

Everything felt like it was moving in slow motion. The man cocked his arm back, ready to throw the ball of fire at him, his own heart encased in ice as his mind flopped first one way and then another, trying to comprehend what was happening. Micah's body moved. He felt like he was watching someone else control him, like a puppeteer had just yanked on his strings. Kicking out, he threw himself backwards, his chill joints protesting the sudden movement. The fireball passed so close to his face that he felt his skin burn and smelt burning hair, whether his eyebrows or fringe of his tonsure he wasn't sure. It shot out the side of the lean-to, sizzling the rain as it went. Micah's foot swept through the fire as it jerked, kicking the burning bundle of sticks directly at his would-be assassin.

The assassin mage screamed and swatted at his eyes. Micah scrambled backwards, out into the rain again. Slipping and sliding, he scrambled to his feet, heart now trying to burst from his chest, pure adrenaline coursing through his blood as he started running blindly into the dark. He gave no thought to the cold. He gave no thought to where he was going. He just ran.

Branches whipped his face in the dark, roots reaching up to try to trip him. Forward he went. Ever forward. He heard the assassin scream in rage behind him as he went, a chill racing down his spine which had nothing to do with the blowing rain.

A whoosh sound reached him and he veered left, just as a fireball flew past him, exploding against a tree, instantly setting it alight despite the rain. His paced slowed as he gawked at the tree which was now encased in flame. It was the roar of rage that pulled him out of his shock and set him running through the night again. The light from the fire had been welcome, but now he found it even harder to see in the dark. He was almost across the break in the trees before he had even realised he had left them behind, sliding to an awkward stop before the building that had risen before him.

A house, his mind belatedly noticed.

Half-way up the slick steps which led to the veranda and entrance, an unnatural force hit him square in the back. Micah had no chance to predict or even react to it. It struck like a solid block of air, hitting him with enough force to send him flying into and through the front door of the house. Bursting through in a spray of wood chips and rain, he tumbled across the entry foyer like a rag doll.

He could barely breathe as he lay on the dust covered floor. Sucking in a gasp of air, Micah, once priest of the Almighty Laran, sobbed, letting the tears flow freely as he said a final silent prayer to whatever god would take him.

Just let it end. He let go. The pain was too much. Not just the physical pain from days in the wild, his tumble down the wet hill, and now being thrown through the door. No. That was horrible, but nothing compared to the pain in his soul, finally knowing that Laran, if he even existed, had abandoned him to his fate.

A floorboard creaked.

Micah looked up to see the silhouette of his killer in the portal where the door had been a moment before. A blast of lightning outside lit his grim face for but a moment. Sighing, he let his head thump back against the floorboards and closed his eyes; he didn't want to see death coming, even though he had accepted it.

'Claudius!'

Micah's eyes shot open at the scream. Behind him, at the top of the staircase stood another figure, wreathed in the orange glow of flame that seemed to completely surround them.

'Valkyr,' Micah gasped.

One of the Allmothers warrior maidens had come to protect him. He couldn't look away from her. She was beauty personified.

He closed his eyes, the image of the flame wreathed woman burned forever into his memory.

Chaos erupted around him.

8

Pain

'Wait,' he hissed at her, but she was already through the door. 'Fuck,' he growled, knees aching at the unexpected movement as he lurched after her.

The mage may have fixed his injured side, but that didn't mean all his other, older pains were gone. In fact, it somehow had made them worse. As if the very knowledge of how easy a mage could mend the human body had somehow made all his old injuries cry out that they should have been fixed like that in the first place.

No time for pain, he chided himself.

Hitting the door with his shoulder as it swung close behind Rinalta, he followed her into the corridor, sword in hand. *Skinny little lass is quick.* She was already at the staircase, moving with a sense of purpose that he couldn't match. Oswald heard the addict, Aliya, squawk something in the room behind him as they left her behind, blue light from the mage's orb flickering out.

'Claudius!' Rinalta screamed from the top of the stairs. Light burst from around the mage, wreathing her in an orange glow of flame as she channelled fire into both hands.

'What's happening?' Aliya asked, catching up to him in the hallway.

'I... lookout!' Grabbing her, Oswald threw Aliya up against the wall and shielded her with his body, wincing at the heat that blasted past them down the corridor. He saw the wallpaper peel off the wall next to them. Aliya trembled under him, and he couldn't help but notice her gauntness. It was like laying on a bundle of sticks. Her blue eyes were wide, like orbs staring at him in shock and fear, but with an edge to them that he recognised and respected, the edge of a survivor.

Wiping sweat from his brow, he looked across as the heat abated. Rinalta was walking down the stairs, one slow step at a time, a shimmering white cone around her shielded her from the plume of flame that was blasting up the stairs, the source of the heat that had just assaulted them and which was now sputtering out.

'You're fucking dead,' Rinalta snarled as her magic shield faded with the flames. She leaped down the stairs and out of Oswald's sight.

'Stay here,' he ordered Aliya, letting her go. She remained standing, back to the wall, trembling slightly but whether from fear or simple drug addled weakness he wasn't sure.

Stopping where the wall ended and the balustrade began, he looked down the stairs to see Rinalta leaping the last four steps, landing next to a figure sprawled on the floor. At first, he thought it was Claudius, but the mage wasn't paying any attention to him, instead all her focus was towards the main door. Rinalta made a throwing motion with her right hand, a blue arc of lighting shooting from her fingertips, making the hair on his neck and arms stand up. It shot through the entrance foyer and through the front door, hitting something he couldn't see and booming loud enough to shake the house and rattle Oswald's teeth in his skull. A shard of ice shot back through the door at Rinalta in reply. She swatted it away with a flame encased hand as easily as swatting a child's hand away. The raven-haired mage stood tall, stepping over the prone figure and advancing with a determination he recognised. It was the determination of a soldier who would give anything to achieve their mission, even if it meant making the ultimate sacrifice, even if it meant taking their entire squad with them. Coupled with the sheer power, more than his mind could have ever imagined before that moment, Oswald felt a thrum of fear run through him. The two mages could tear down the very building around them as easily as he berated a green lad stepping onto a parade ground for the first time. The wall rattled next to him and one of the faded paintings down the hall fell, the thump of the solid frame loud enough to reach him even over the noise of the magic battle below.

'Rinalta!' He yelled down at her, hoping to remind her that other lives were on the line. She continued her advance, ignoring him and flinging two more fireballs out into the storm as she did so.

Wincing, he started down the stairs after her. As a young soldier, he had hated going up staircases, and not just because it had normally meant he was lugging something up them for a preening noble, but simply because of the effort. Young soldiers have an aversion to doing more than the absolute bare minimum amount of effort. Now, going downstairs was the hard part. The impact of each step set his knees aching, every step an effort to keep stiff joints moving.

Rinalta disappeared through the shattered front door as he reached the foyer. The man on the floor was alive, panting with wide eyes staring up at the roof as if lost in his own mind. Oswald's first thought was to follow her out the door and help her fight Claudius; not that he actually knew who the fuck Claudius was. It was an instinct to protect a squad mate. An instinct that went down to his very bones, but why he felt it for a woman he had just met he wasn't sure. Maybe because she had healed him? Logic won out over instinct as another plume of flame shot past the door, lighting the storm outside.

'Hey,' he said, kneeling next to the man on the floor and shaking him. 'Hey!' he yelled.

The man blinked. 'Valkyr,' he answered. 'The Valkyr are here.'

'Yeah, whatever,' Oswald answered, wondering if the man was cracked in the head. 'In case you haven't noticed, there are two mages pegging fire and lightning at each other just out there, so if you wanna live, get your arse up and move.'

The booming was moving closer again, light and thunder of the fight moving towards the entrance of the dilapidated house.

'Move!' Oswald commanded. Grabbing the nut-bag by a fraying sleeve of his robe, he used his bulk to drag him towards the stairs.

Rinalta's opponent burst through the entrance. His plain clothes were soaked through, cloak smouldering where a chunk of it had been burned away in the fight. Oswald saw the attacker's eyes flash as he noticed the two of them making their way to the stairs, trying to escape the onslaught of power. He recognised that look.

'Down!' Throwing himself forward, he tackled the addled stranger, sending them back to the dusty floor in a tangle of arms and legs. An arc of lightning passed through the spot where they had been only a moment before. Oswald felt the power of it as it passed over him. All the hair on his body stood on end, from the hair on the back of his hands to the short-cropped stubble on top of his head. The little man cried out as Oswald landed on top of him, a whoosh of air cutting it short. Rolling, Oswald tried to find his sword, lost in the tumble, knowing he would need to fight off their assailant alone at this point.

There!

The blade had slid across the foyer. All the way to where the enemy mage stood, hand rising to shoot another bolt of energy at them.

Fuck.

He had always known he would die in battle. And yet, he had expected it to be from the thrust of a blade, hopefully one that would end it swiftly but knowing it was just as likely to be a slow, painful, and gruesome end. Oswald couldn't help but wonder if death by lightning would be swift.

The enemy mage's head jerked sideways as another figure burst through the door, fire launching from it as it came. It was Rinalta, once again wreathed in the orange glow of flame and fury. A translucent shield shot up around the other mage a split second before the fireball struck. It exploded on the shield, sending gouts of flame through the room, one hitting the balustrade of the stairs with a deafening boom. By the time Oswald's eyes cleared, the enemy mage was gone.

Rinalta let out a howl of rage and frustration, fists clenched as she bent double, forcing the noise out until her breath was spent.

Oswald got to his feet, stumbling over the other man as he did so, ignoring the click and subsequent spark of pain that shot through his knee at the awkward movement. He scooped up his sword and stood ready to fight. 'Where is he?' he asked, eyes darting around the room.

'Gone,' Rinalta answered. She stood in the middle of the room, head hanging, looking deflated. Oswald knew it wasn't just from the exhaustion. 'He must have had a way-rune.'

'Valkyr,' a voice said over his shoulder. It was the man he had saved. Oswald looked at him, deciding he was likely some sort of religious fanatic based on his robe and tonsure.

There was a madness in his eyes. His unblinking gaze was fixed on Rinalta, although she hadn't noticed yet.

'Who the fuck are you?' Oswald asked.

The man blinked several times, looking at Oswald as if he had only just noticed he was there. 'My name is Micah,' he said softly, eyes darting back to Rinalta. 'I was a priest of Laran, but now, after seeing you, mighty and beautiful Valkyr,' he knelt before Rinalta, 'I will never doubt the power of the Allmother again.'

Rinalta's mouth hung open, hand half-way to her face to brush back a lock of hair that had fluttered free. 'What?'

'I'm sorry, have I offended you, Valkyr?' The man's face was downturned.

Rinalta looked across at Oswald as he shrugged. 'Apparently you are a mythological warrior of the Allmother.'

She burst out laughing. Micah looked up at her, pained look on his face. 'I'm no Valkyr.'

'But... the vision... I...' he trailed off, brows drawn tight.

'Reckon that Claudius fellow is coming back?' Oswald asked.

'Unfortunately not,' Rinalta answered, mood turning serious again. She held out a hand, conjuring another of the blue orbs.

'Let's get back upstairs then,' he suggested, yanking Micah to his feet by a shoulder. 'Come on priest.'

9

Vengeance

The blue light in her palm flickered as the connection with her Centre faltered, her mana reserve almost completely depleted. Oswald looked back at her over a broad shoulder, halting with one foot on the step, the stranger leaning heavily on him as if he was about to pass out.

Breathe, she told herself, flashing the soldier a wane smile. It was the best she could do given the circumstances. Healing Oswald had taken a lot out of her; she had never been particularly good at healing magic. If the healing had tired her out, her battle with the betrayer, Claudius, had left her exhausted beyond anything she could remember in her life. She had been pushed at the College of Rel, of course. Pushed so hard she had thought she could feel herself about to shatter right down to a basic level, fracturing even her Centre. She hadn't. Instead, they had told her, that like a diamond, she had been compressed and was now more valuable, and powerful because of it. She didn't feel compressed or powerful right then. She just felt tired, all the way down to her bones.

'Come on,' Oswald said, shoving the man ahead of him, 'We should be safe upstairs again. You look like you could use some rest.' Rinalta wasn't sure if he was speaking to her or the stranger.

Her mind floated like a feather blown by the wind. She followed Oswald up the stairs, body moving without conscious thought, each step feeling like she was stepping over a mountain, each step feeling like her body couldn't possibly go on. What would her master think if he could see her now? Would the roses be in bloom back home? Someone should really invent some sort of crane mechanism to lift people, so they didn't have to walk upstairs.

'You coming?'

Rinalta started, turning to look down the corridor where Oswald and Aliya awaited her, standing before the entrance to the room they were occupying. She had been standing at the top of the stairs, staring at the floor in front of her.

'Yes. Sorry.' She shook her head and took a deep breath, working through a basic concentration activity in an attempt to focus her mind. Picturing a closed flower, she tried to visualise each petal opening, one at a time to reveal the beautiful whole. It was a basic exercise, one she had not struggled with since she had been a novice in the College, at least until today anyway. By the time she reached the open door, now sitting even more ajar than it had previously, she had succeeded in opening the flower, although a sheen of sweat had broken out on her forehead at the effort. Stepping into the room, she felt more alert, although her thoughts still felt like they were dragging themselves through a mud pit.

'Sit down before you fall,' Oswald growled at the stranger, half shoving him to the floor. From Rinalta's cursory inspection of him, he didn't appear to have any physical injuries and yet he was moving slower and with more hesitancy than even she was.

'What's your name?' Aliya asked. 'I'm Aliya, and this is Oswald and Rinalta,' she introduced them in a rush. Aliya stared at the man with an intense fascination that unsettled Rinalta. Perhaps it was a result of her foggy, exhausted mind, but she got the feeling that the seraphim addict was somehow peering into him, weighing his soul. The man probably would have been unsettled by the attention, if he had noticed it, that is. Instead, he was staring at Rinalta, eyes wide and mouth working dumbly.

'Are you alright? Injured?' Rinalta asked, sitting with him on her right and Oswald on her left. Aliya sat across from her, all together making a small little circle within which she placed her flickering blue orb. Her fire aura during the fight with Claudius had kept her almost completely dry, but the priest was completely soaked through and smelled like a mouldy piece of bread dipped in swamp water.

'Injured? Yes, uh… I mean no. I mean, uh, my name's Micah. I don't mean to offend you, Valkyr, or the Allmother.'

A shiver ran down her spine and even in her muddled state, she noticed Oswald and Aliya stiffen at the mention of the Allmother. Micah was staring at her with a scary intensity, a combination of divine ecstasy and unabashed lust. His eyes seemed to crawl over her in an unconscious way, pausing on her chest and hips, making her self-conscious at how her shirt and pants pulled tight in those areas.

'I'm not a Valkyr,' Rinalta said. She tugged at her shirt, trying to loosen it from around her chest. 'Just a mage. I don't even believe in Valkyrs or the Allmother.' Micah's lip curled in disgust at the mention of being a mage, passing so quick Rinalta doubted it had even been there. 'Why was Claudius chasing you? And what are you doing out here?' Oswald and Aliya shared a glance but seemed content to leave the talking to Rinalta.

'A mage,' Micah muttered under his breath. He blinked twice at her and hunched deeper into his soaked robe before answering. 'Claudius? I didn't even know his name. He invited me to his fire, offering sanctuary, then told me I should never have escaped, that the darklings failed to kill me.'

'Darklings?' Oswald asked sharply. 'What do you mean, darklings?'

'It sounds like madness, I'm sure,' he said with a half-hearted chuckle.

'Not to us,' Aliya assured him, patting him gently on the arm.

'Why don't you start at the beginning,' Rinalta suggested. Her eyes felt like they weighed a ton, and she had no desire to go back and forth all night. The quicker he told his story, the quicker she could rest.

Micah looked her over again, head cocked slightly to one side. His story started haltingly but slowly built into a coherent tale. The village he had been tending had been destroyed by darklings, and yet he had somehow been spared, presumably because he had been unconscious at the time of the attack and therefore taken for dead. Rinalta was not comfortable with his vague explanation of being unconscious; he was clearly omitting something important. His explanation of his days in the woods and his meeting with Claudius were clearer, although tinged with fear. The story was completed as he described how he was thrown through the front door of the house by a blast of power from Claudius, only to be rescued by what he thought was a Valkyr. Rinalta noted a hint of disappointment as he spoke of this.

'You probably think I'm mad,' he finished quietly, eyes going vacant as he hugged himself.

'No,' Oswald said, voice firm but not ungentle. 'We have seen the darklings as well and had visions of the Allmother.' Aliya was vigorously bobbing her head to this.

'For the record,' Rinalta added, 'I have not, and am still having a hard time believing a fairytale monster is rampaging across the countryside.' Exhaustion was cracking her veneer of control. Control, Master Gerard had always told her, was what separated mages from regular people. Control over self and control over the primordial power of mana. *What would you think of me now?* 'I also don't believe there is some deity taking a hand in what is happening here. We are the master of our destiny, some people just have more control over their lives than others and the easy answer is to blame destiny, or this god or that god. It's more reassuring to believe that an all-seeing, all-knowing figure has decided that your life will suck rather than just admitting that you are too afraid to take risks to make it better.'

The silence as her diatribe halted was thick. The other three all sat, looking at the dusty floor in between them, unsure how to respond and shifting awkwardly.

'I was an adherent of Laran,' Micah finally said. 'I spent years hoping he would reveal whatever plan he had for me. I struggled against his edicts, striving to be an acolyte worthy of his regard. I now realise that I was a fool.'

Rinalta held back a sigh of relief. 'I'm glad you agree with me,' she said quietly. Her embarrassment abated slightly, although her cheeks still flushed hot. She couldn't remember the last time she had lost control like that. For so long she had kept her tongue leashed, living by the lessons her master had instilled, doing her best not to alienate those around her as she had done as a child and young woman.

'I don't agree with you,' Micah retorted calmly. This time the flash of disgust was obvious, causing Rinalta to flush hot and break out in a sweat. 'I now understand that my faith in Laran was misplaced but am coming to accept that my vision of the Allmother was real. I don't yet understand what that means, or what the Allmother wants, but I believe that she is real and has brought, at least us three,' he waved a hand at himself, Aliya, and Oswald, 'together for a purpose. I simply wish the gods I pray to would answer clearly for once. Why won't they answer my prayers? Why won't they tell me why I –' he cut off.

The awkward silence grew thicker.

Shuffling, Rinalta could tell from their body language that Oswald and Aliya agreed with the former priest. Micah was looking at her again, eyes ranging over her body and face as if he was drinking her in somehow. Her flesh crawled.

'It doesn't really matter right now,' Oswald said. Rinalta was grateful, not just for breaking the tension but also for breaking Micah's uncomfortable attention for her. 'We all need sleep. We can discuss what we are going to do in the morning, even if that something is go our separate ways.'

'Good idea,' Aliya agreed enthusiastically. She was looking at the soldier with wide eyes and Rinalta knew the girl would be leaving with him no matter where he was going. It didn't take the power of premonition to see she was smitten.

No meaningless goodnights were shared between them as they all sought to get as comfortable as they could on the hard, cold floors. Micah lay down where he had been sitting, facing towards her. Trying to be circumspect, Rinalta shuffled as far from him as she could and lay down with her back to him, wrapping herself in her cloak and using her pack as a pillow. Despite her cloak being a fabric barrier between them, she could still feel his eyes on her. Not caring if the others had gotten comfortable yet - there was still some shuffling and groaning - she cut off the mana flow to the flickering blue light, letting the room descend into darkness. Goosebumps prickled her flesh, sleep a distant thought as an icy chill ran down her spine. *Is he still looking at me?* she wondered to herself. Rinalta wasn't sure what rattled her the most; his eyes creeping all over her or the surety and zeal with which he had spoken. He may have been a priest of Laran only days before, but he had shifted that faith wholly onto the Allmother because of a single vision. That kind of fervor could be dangerous. And his strange questions had been tinged with a… madness? She wasn't sure if that was the right way to describe it. How many history books had she read at the college in which one faith wiped out another, simply because it decided that it was the only faith that men should follow and that all others were an affront to it? Religion, in her mind at least, was incompatible with peace. Thoughts like this rattled across her exhausted mind, flitting in and out, a constant stream of consciousness without direction that did nothing but delay her sleep. Eventually, exhaustion won out and she slipped into a fitful sleep. Vague dreams of dark shadow creatures and angry mobs calling her a heretic made her toss and turn.

She ran from the mob, torches waving behind her, turning the night sky into a warm orange glow. It was the glow of righteous fury. They followed her through the woods, screaming incoherently behind her, chasing, chasing, chasing her deeper into the darkness where shadow creatures awaited her. She could hear them skittering through the trees. She could see their red eyes in the dark. The mob following her did not seem to notice. Something snagged her foot, and she fell face down in the mud, rolling as the screams of rage closed around her. Glowing torches were waved in her face, blinding her with their light, although there was no heat in them. Waving her arms wildly, Rinalta tried to bat them away, hands grabbing at her, pulling from every direction.

Rinalta screamed.

'Rinalta!' a worried voice called.

Only one hand was on her now, shaking instead of pulling. She sat bolt upright, panting for breath, slick sweat coating her. Reaching into her Centre, the configuration for a fireball instinctually leaped into her hand, lighting up the dusty room with its orange glow.

'It's me! It's Aliya,' the soft voice said, hand disappearing from her shoulder. 'You were having a nightmare.'

Rinalta blinked. There was no angry mob standing over her, just a scared, emaciated seraphim addict squatting beside her.

'Put that fucking light out,' Oswald hissed across the room.

Looking across, she saw the grizzled soldier kneeling next to the grime covered window, one leg skewed out to the side awkwardly. She was going to ask why until she saw his drawn sword and instead complied without a word.

'Darklings,' Aliya whispered. Even in the dim light of the room, she could see that Aliya's eyes were wide with barely restrained fear. Survivor she may be, but whatever was out in the dark terrified her.

Rinalta wiped the sweat off her brow with the back of her hand and rose into a half squat, making her way around the terrified addict towards Oswald. It was only when she was halfway across that she wondered about the priest. A quick glance showed him huddling in the corner near the door, knees drawn up to his chin, eyes closed and lips working furiously as he muttered under his breath in prayer. Stopping next to Oswald, she kneeled by the window, squinting to see through the grime that came from years of neglect. It was still dark outside although Rinalta thought it must have been getting close to dawn. Wiping crusty sleep from the corner of her eye, she was ready to call them all a bunch of nervous sheep running around a pen at the first shadow that flittered in the night. She was going to say that, she was sick of squinting, but as she turned to speak, she saw the shadow in the night for herself. It was barely more than that. Just a shape in the darkness, moving between the trees that surrounded the dilapidated mansion. Frozen in place, her mind tried to rationalise what she had seen, to place the shape of the normal, everyday woodland creature that she had surely just seen. But there was no creature she could think of that would make a shape such as that nor send a thrum of primordial fear through her at just a glance.

'Darkling,' she whispered under her breath.

Micah squeaked, huddling deeper into the far corner.

Wanting to find some way to prove, if only to herself, that she hadn't seen the thing, Rinalta rubbed her eyes and leaned closer to the window. Another three shadows flitted between the trees. They all had the same shape, invoked the same dread within her, melting away any illusion she tried to cling to as her heart beat faster.

'Maybe they'll just go past,' Aliya whispered hopefully.

Micah squeaked again. 'No. They're hunting me.'

Rinalta shot Oswald a glance which he returned with a shrug. Years of training helped him keep his cool, but it was obvious that he was just as frightened as the rest of them, that the darklings gave him the same sense of dread. And yet, he was steady. Rinalta knew she could depend on him if it came to a fight with the creatures; the other two though, she was not so sure of.

A thud echoed through the house, seeming to reverberate through the very floorboards, dust falling from the roof in a cloud. A piercing scream followed the thud, loud enough that they all covered their ears, Oswald dropping his blade. Rinalta's heart stopped for a beat and then pounded, pounded as if it was trying to break free of her chest and escape the unnatural creature and its bone chilling scream. A second scream followed it, layering on top of the first. She had to clench her legs to stop herself from pissing her pants. Whatever was now thumping up the stairs towards them was no woodland beast. A small part of her said it could not be a darkling, that they weren't real, they were just fairytales to scare children. That was just a small part of her though. The rest knew exactly what was about to burst in on them, even if she didn't know exactly what it would look like.

Oswald scooped up his sword and shoved Aliya behind him as he took a fighting stance in the centre of the room. He glanced at Rinalta as she took a spot just behind him and to the left. Fireball configurations fluttered to life in her hands, and she nodded to him, face tight with grim determination. She spared a glance for Micah, still cowering in the corner, but had no time to do anything about him.

The darkling slammed into the room, door ripping outwards with a smash that was lost as the foul creature screamed again.

Rinalta threw both fireballs at the same time.

10

Addiction

Thump, thump, thump.

Something large was bounding up the stairs, shaking the room and making dust fall from the mouldy roof.

Thump, thump, thump.

Her heartbeat in her chest, the sound pounding in her ears almost loud enough to drown out the sound of certain death coming up the stairs towards them.

Thump, thump, thump.

I wish I had some seraphim. The thought passed through her mind, an irresistible craving welling up in the pit of her stomach, followed by disgust. *How can you be thinking of that shit at a time like this?*

Aliya felt a trickle of piss wet her undergarments before she could clench and stop it. She didn't care. The number of times she had pissed herself while lost in the addictive euphoria of seraphim had desensitised her to the smell or worry about what people thought of her. Heat flushed into her gaunt cheeks though as she looked at the brawny man standing before her. Oswald had pushed her behind him, a little roughly, but still, no one had ever cared enough to try to protect her like that. He wasn't much to look at; a far cry from the noble warrior she had dreamed of as a child, but she wasn't exactly a beauty these days.

What the hell am I thinking?

Thump, thump, thump.

A piercing shriek had her covering her ears, the clatter of Oswald's sword as it fell to the floor lost in the noise.

She couldn't help the scream that escaped her as the darkling burst through the door, wood splintering as it rent its way into the room. Two bright orbs flew from beside her. Looking across, Rinalta was standing like a Valkyr, dark hair fluttering around her head, another set of fireballs manifesting in the palms of her hands.

Another shriek drew her attention back to the door. The burning darkling was shrieking wildly, talons pawing at the flames as it fell backwards through the door and into the hallway. A burning pile of shit would have smelt better than the stench its scorching flesh made. Aliya let herself believe, just for a second, that it was over. A second shadow launched itself over the burning darkling and into the dimly lit room. Someone screamed. At first, Aliya thought it was her, then realised it had been the priest, Micah, now huddling against the wall behind them.

Oswald roared and charged forward, scooping up his sword.

'Oswald!' Aliya yelled.

He slammed into the creature with a sickening crunch. More fireballs flew past them towards the door, shrieks telling her another darkling had been struck by them.

Oswald was furiously slashing at the shadow, ducking its talons as they flashed with the light of the fireballs. He grunted, blocking another blow that would have filleted him. Air whooshed from his lungs as the next blow struck him in the chest, sending him flying backwards to slam into the wall.

Aliya wanted to scream, to run to him, to do anything, but the shadow looming up before her froze her. Her blood felt like ice in her veins, stomach churning and bladder loosening again. Her already quivering legs almost gave out. It pulled itself to full height, almost twice her size, with long gangly limbs, razor sharp talons at their ends. It had an elongated, oval shaped head that seemed too large, giant ruby eyes glowing in the darkness. She couldn't make out any other details, it seemed to be encased in a thin cloud of shadows, but somehow she knew there would be razor sharp teeth in its mouth, perfect for shredding rangy little seraphim addicts into pieces. The ruby eyes seemed to pierce right through her. She felt impaled on that gaze; pinned to the spot, unable to move even if she wanted to.

A flash of orange blurred past her, the heat singing her arm before it slammed into the shadow looming before her. The creature screamed. The sound pierced her head like a spike. Her stare was broken as she clasped her head in her hands. As the noise abated somewhat, she saw the burning darkling step towards her, talon no longer trying to put out the conflagration its body had become. Rather it was raised to strike at her, to disembowel her with its dying breath.

A roar, this time from behind her, was all the warning she had. She was flung to the side, crashing into Rinalta in a tangle of arms and legs. Oswald kicked the creature in its chest, forcing it back, heedless of the flames, swinging his sword in furious arcs, venting his fury in a flurry of blows and screams. Aliya heard Rinalta curse, pushing her sideways so the mage could regain her feet. Aliya was still laying on her side when Oswald stepped forward and plunged his sword into the darkling's chest, flames dancing around him and the smell of burnt flesh joining the rank smell of cooking monster.

'Move!' Rinalta screamed into the tumult.

Oswald stumbled back, losing his footing and crashing backwards onto his hindquarters.

A burst of force, visible only from the dust that it pushed, burst from the mage's hands, slamming into the burning darkling, finally silencing its scream as it was shot backwards. It struck one of the grimy windows, smashing the glass and taking a chunk of the wall with it as it fell into the storm.

'Allmother save me.' Micah was huddled in the corner, hands clasped, muttering prayers. 'Let her light shine on me and protect me.'

Oswald hissed and growled.

'Oswald!' Aliya cried, fighting to stand on weak legs.

The grizzled warrior was holding his hands before him, sitting in the middle of the room, teeth showing in a grimace of pain. Kneeling next to him, Aliya could see his hands were covered in burns, skin red and black, heat blisters already bursting.

'Rinalta,' Aliya said, getting the mage's attention. 'Oswald needs to be healed.'

The raven-haired woman sighed and slumped, shaking her head. 'I can't.'

'What?'

'It's fine,' Oswald said through gritted teeth. 'I've been through worse.'

'But she can heal you.'

'She's exhausted,' Oswald said with a shake of his head. 'And she's our best defence. It'll be better for us all is she has enough energy to fight off the next wave of those things.'

'Next wave?' Micah squeaked from the corner.

Aliya looked at Oswald. There was no question that her shaking was now from fear.

'There'll be more,' Rinalta said. 'We need to get out of here.'

'Guessing you believe us about the darklings now?' Oswald asked with a snort.

'Hard to argue with that,' she said, pointing at the smoking corpse in the corridor. 'Come on, let's move.'

Aliya helped Oswald to his feet, gripping his thick upper arms, careful not to brush his hands. He seemed to be moving in fits and jerks; obviously more than his hands were in pain. She thought of his scarred body and wondered how many of the old injuries were now plaguing him after fighting off the darkling. It was unlikely that he had done it just for her, yet still, a part of her couldn't help but think he had been protecting her.

'You coming, priest?' Rinalta asked over her shoulder, letting Aliya and Oswald step out into the hallway in front of her.

Looking back, Aliya watched Micah scurry to his feet and run towards them. She wasn't sure why but seeing the priest shaking in fear shored up her courage, feet feeling more solid underneath her.

'We need some clean, cold water for your hands,' Aliya said to Oswald. The house was eerily silent except for the sound of rain being blown past its eaves. She could hear the dusty floorboards underfoot creaking, a cold draft blowing through the halls, likely through the broken front door. Rinalta took the lead again, taking them back to the main staircase and down into the entry hall. As they were crossing the open hall, stepping over the broken door sitting on the tile floor, a shriek rang out through the night, stilling them all.

The courage she thought she had found fled. Ruby eyes flashed outside the door, glowing through the darkness and rain.

'Move!' Rinalta yelled.

Oswald reacted faster than her, turning left, all but dragging her down a hallway on the ground floor as she clung to his upper arm. He moved with a semi-limping hobble. Old injuries were clearly an issue, and yet, she was still puffing when they reached the end of the narrow corridor. She thought it must have been a servant's corridor based on the size and lack of ostentation. Mould stains covered the plaster walls, rain blowing in through the smashed window at the end of the hall. Hitting the door with his shoulder, Oswald dragged her through the portal. If it wasn't for his solid frame stopping her, she would have tumbled down the stairs into the dark basement below as he slammed the door shut behind them.

'Downstairs, see if there's a way out,' Oswald ordered.

Aliya moved as quickly as she dared, placing each foot on the step below, ensuring it was there, before taking her wait from the step above. She almost slipped several times, fear of the creatures pushing her for speed, fear of the dark below slowing her down. A wet earthy smell overwhelmed her. It wasn't the clean smell of fresh tilled earth, but rather a dank metallic smell, both mouldy and rotting at the same time. She heard Oswald thumping something back up the stairs behind her as her foot met the soft, earthy ground at the bottom of the stairs.

'Not sure how long that'll hold them,' he whispered in her ear, making her jump.

'There's no light,' she said, voice quivering.

'Here.'

She heard him moving through the dark. Turning towards the sound, she saw his silhouette, lit by a tiny square of light coming through a window near the ceiling. A single window, barely the size of a loaf of bread, sitting at ground level outside was the only other access point to the room, an access point too small for even her gaunt frame to fit through. Moving carefully, she joined Oswald in the tiny patch of faded light. They stood in silence, listening to the storm, straining, waiting for the flimsy door to the basement to be shattered inwards.

Moments passed.

Aliya placed her hand on Oswald's arm, feeling the bulky muscles tense underneath his shirt. She stepped into him, careful not to brush his hands, moving both her own hands onto his chest. His arms lifted, carefully encircling her, hands held out so only his forearms touched her. She could feel his heart pounding in his chest. Aliya didn't know if it was from fear or her touch. She wasn't sure why her own was pounding anymore. Rising onto the tips of her toes, hands sliding up his chest to wrap around his neck, she planted her lips on his. At first he didn't respond, then, he pulled her in tight to his body, a low rumble coming from his chest as his tongue slipped into her mouth. She reached down and undid his pants for him, his own hands all but useless right then, before hiking up her skirts and pulling down her threadbare panties.

It was ridiculous. She knew it was. Knew that at any moment a darkling would likely burst in and kill them both. That only made her desire for him burn hotter. She pushed him back onto a crate, sitting against the earth wall of the basement, forcing him to sit. He let her take charge. She'd never done that before. Of the countless men she had bedded with, Oswald was the first to let her set the pace, to do more than just lay on her back and take whatever the man desired. Everything about the moment heightened her desire. The death just outside the door, the control, his inability to touch her with his burnt hands.

She couldn't help the moan that came out of her as she slid down on top of him. He groaned along with her, which only made her climax all the sweeter.

11

Lust

Micah ran.

The screams were right behind him, the others were already dead, he was sure of it. They had probably been foolish enough to try to fight the hell beasts again. Micah knew there was no fighting such creatures.

But he was still alive. The Allmother must still have a plan for him. He didn't know the correct way to venerate her, but surely she would accept his silent prayers of thanks as he stumbled down the dilapidated corridor, heart in his throat. A half-broken window was ahead of him, broken doors along each side leading to other rooms. He didn't know which room to pick. He couldn't shut any of the doors and the darklings were behind him. Everything seemed to be happening too fast for him, and yet it felt like he was wading through mud, barely able to move. Which door should he choose.

'The window!' A voice behind him screamed. It was the Valkyr, Rinalta. His heart beat a little faster at the thought of her before the reality sunk back into his mind.

The window? What could she possibly mean. His legs kept moving him towards it, close enough now to notice there had once been a pattern on the now threadbare hangings that fluttered in the wind.

A yelp escaped him as something hit him from behind. They had him. The darklings would tear him apart and send his immortal soul to the abyss.

Only, he didn't hit the floor. There was no weight on top of him.

Rather, he went flying, straight for the window. His body twisted and his right shoulder connected with the frame, sending him crashing through it, the force pushing him disappearing as soon as he hit. Mind reeling, he rolled through the mud before sliding to a stop. Rain pelted down on his face, soaking him in an instant.

'Get up you idiot,' Rinalta yelled.

Still dazed, he propped himself up on one arm just in time to see her vaulting through the shattered window.

'D... Did you just?' He pointed weakly at the window; certain she had just used him like a battering ram to make an exit.

'Move!' she screamed, grabbing him by one arm and hauling him to his feet.

The piercing shriek of a darkling as it thumped through the house got him moving faster than he thought possible.

Slipping in the mud, he grabbed Rinalta's arm, almost pulling her over in his bid to escape the horrors that still chased them. The darkness made it near impossible to see as they scrambled. The bursts of lightning were too far apart to provide any real illumination, thick clouds blocking the moonlight, and rain sheeting down in a heavy downpour. Still gripping Rinalta's forearm, Micah trusted her sense of direction more than his own at that moment. His last foray into the woods was a disaster and she was moving with confidence.

He'd expected to start tripping over roots. Expected tree branches to start snaring him as they ran. Instead, his Valkyr stopped, yanking her arm free of his grip.

'Inside,' she said, barely audible over the rain, pushing him forward.

His foot caught on something, sending him stumbling, air rushing from his lungs as he hit the soft packed earth hard. Something thumped. Micah wheezed.

'How do those things track?' Rinalta muttered. 'Fuck.' There was a thud then a sliding sound.

Micah blinked and took deep breaths, only now noticing the rain was gone, although the pounding of it sounded on a roof. They were inside somewhere. He blinked, trying to see his surroundings with little success.

'Where are we? Did we escape those things?' His voice came out as a croaky whine.

'Some sort of tool shed,' Rinalta answered, sounding distracted. 'They didn't follow us out the window... But why?' The question came out as a whisper.

He pulled himself to his feet slowly, arms waving out in front of himself in the dark, making sure he didn't crash into anything. His foot scraped on the floor as he took a step and finally realised he was missing a shoe, lost somewhere in the mad scramble to escape. His heart was still pounding. He twitched at every scrape, every twist in the darkness; calling the moving dark shadows was too generous.

'Surely they can track us,' Rinalta muttered.

Micah moved towards the sound of her voice, barely audible over the thudding of rain on the roof of the shed.

'What are you doing?' She hissed as Micah stumbled into her. He almost lost his footing again, wrapping his arms around her in the dark. 'Get off me!' She pushed him in the chest.

He stumbled back a step, catching his balance and holding out his arms to the sides. Heat flushed through him, enough to stop the shivering that had started as soon as he fell into the downpour. The press of her body against his own, the curve of her hips as he had wrapped his arms around her, the warmth of her breath on his neck.

A shiver ran through his body which had nothing to do with the cold.

Allmother forgive my sins, he prayed silently. Laran had never helped curb his unnatural urges towards women, and so far the Allmother had not either, although he had not prayed to her for long.

He felt his manhood swell. He prayed. Asking, no, begging the Allmother to take this curse from him.

'Stop your muttering,' Rinalta hissed at him. 'They're outside.'

Micah hadn't intended to vocalise his prayers in the first place. He stepped towards Rinalta, careful this time, careful not to make a noise lest the monster discover them, but also careful not to touch her again. Touching her, feeling her body had been beyond his wildest imaginings. If he felt her again...

Don't think about that, he cursed himself.

'They're searching around the house,' Rinalta whispered, somehow knowing he had joined her in the dark, her warm breath caressing his cheek. He couldn't see a thing in the dark yet that didn't seem to affect Rinalta. 'I can't figure out how they hunt. Smell maybe? Could the rain be masking our scent?'

Her voice was so silken smooth, delicate like a butterfly flapping its wings, yet powerful like a gale. Micah was barely aware of what she was saying. He could feel the heat coming from her body, imagined the steam that must be coming off her wet clothes as her body warmed the fabric. Thinking of her wet clothes clinging to her body forced a shudder through him. Micah shuffled closer to her.

'They're leaving,' Rinalta said. 'Heading into the forest. What...' she trailed off.

Micah shuffled closer to her again, close enough to brush up against her.

Perhaps all this is the Allmothers design, he wondered to himself. *Perhaps she put me here, in this shed with Rinalta, not to test me but to tell me my urges are her will.*

His blood was stirring. The thought of Rinalta, a Valkyr made manifest in his mind, being given to him like this. By this point, he was sure she was more than a filthy mage and heretic.

He stepped forward and grabbed her round the waist, pulling her into himself, puckering lips seeking her own in the dark.

'Hey! What are you -'

They tripped, going down in a tangle of sodden limbs. Micah landed on top of her, feeling her legs open as he pushed up against her, the whoosh of breath cutting off her protests. *Yes,* he thought, *this is definitely the Allmother's will.* Reaching down, he hiked up his robe, now a bare remnant of the noble garment it was only days ago. Rinalta's arms pawed at him in the dark but seemed to be more beckoning than protesting; surely if she didn't want this she would hit him harder than that? He found the laces of her breeches and started tugging at them, impatient now that he understood his purpose here, understood that this was his divine mandate.

Years of resisting, years of suppressing his urges in the name of the false god Laran. All of that was about to be undone. He was going to get his release, and with a Valkyr of all women.

He tugged harder.

Why won't her damn pants just come down already.

Micah grinded down on her again, moaning at the promise of what was to come.

12

Pain

Oswald tugged up his pants, fumbling in the dark to redo his laces, fire in his joints reasserting itself now that the pleasure was gone.

Shame washed through him. What had he been thinking? Here they were, trapped in the basement of a crumbling building, and he had given into base urges and taken advantage of the young addict. It had probably happened to her many times before, but that was no excuse for his behaviour.

He pulled his laces tight as best he could, opening his mouth to whisper an apology.

Aliya placed her delicate hand on his cheek, covering his lips with a finger. 'Thank you,' she whispered.

His hands went limp at his sides. *What could she mean? Thank you?* 'I... Uh.'

'It sounds like they're gone,' she whispered. Aliya found his hand in the dark and held it, making him hiss in pain, although he did not pull away. 'Sorry, I forgot about your hands.'

The throbbing, burning pain reasserted itself at her touch. He'd suffered many different types of pain before, but burning had to be one of the worst. It was relentless. There was no way to avoid it, no position you could shift to or way to compensate that would ease your suffering even for a moment. And yet, for those few moments with this woman, wrapped in her ecstasy, the pain had been driven from him. Not just the burns, but all his pain.

'We should wait a little longer, just to be sure,' he whispered back. Aliya showed no inclination to discuss what they had done in the dark together, so he decided to set it aside for now.

'Do you think Rinalta and Micah made it to safety?'

He sighed. 'I don't know. They ran in the opposite direction.'

'We should go find them, try to help them.' The girl – and she was just a girl compared to him – sidled up next to him, putting her head on his shoulder as he leaned against a crate.

'Even if I still had my sword, I couldn't hold it. We would be worse than useless to Rinalta, we would be a liability. It's best if we stay put for now.' Oswald could practically feel the girl's eyes on him, even in the dark. They bored into him like a spear point. He shuffled, shifting on the crate, painfully aware of her warm body beside him.

'They could be hurt,' she whispered.

Stifling a groan, Oswald stood, pulling away from her. 'Alright,' he sighed. 'We go slow and you stay behind me. If I tell you to run, you run and you don't stop. Do you understand?'

'I understand.'

He had lost a lot of soldiers over the years, pretty much all his friends, but he would be damned before he lost this girl.

They inched their way through the dark basement back towards the rickety stairs. Oswald placed a foot on the first step, a stabbing pain lancing through his knee as it took his weight. *Bloody Spics*, he thought to himself. The campaign into Spicland had been particularly vicious, leaving him with far fewer friends and too many new pains. Aliya was breathing heavily behind him as he reached the door. How it had held against the darklings he would never know. Taking a deep breath, he placed his shoulder against it, working the latch and letting it creep open ever so slightly.

'Anything?' Aliya hissed after a moment.

Oswald paused. 'Nothing.'

Pushing the door fully open, Oswald stepped hesitantly out into the shadowy hallway. The creatures had always seemed to melt into the shadows, as if they were made from them. Oswald eyed every dark patch with suspicion before letting Aliya follow him up out of the basement. She reached for his hand again as they started back towards the entry foyer together, but grabbed his shoulder instead, remembering his burnt hands. He had no idea what he would do if they ran into another darkling. He had no weapon and could barely clench his fist without doubling over in agony.

'It's empty,' Aliya said too loudly.

The foyer was completely empty, the only sound the rain pounding against the ground coming through the broken door. 'Something's not right,' Oswald muttered. Dust and decaying furniture were the only smells. The rain hadn't yet penetrated the gloom of the manor; the shadows still held sway here, nature had not yet reclaimed it. 'This way.' He led Aliya down the corridor he was fairly sure Rinalta and Micah had run down.

Something moved at the end of the corridor. Aliya's hand clenched tightly on his shoulder.

'Just a curtain,' he whispered to her, feeling her grip soften at his words. A small part of him marveled at how quickly this slip of a girl was trusting him, a complete stranger.

'What's moving it?'

'Just the wind, the window...' he trailed off, continuing down the corridor.

Aliya shuffled along with him. 'What is it?'

'This was only broken recently, and it was broken outwards.' The shards of glass that were still clinging desperately to the frame were pointed out into the stormy night. Rain was blowing in through the window yet even in the dark, Oswald could see there was no water damage on the inside.

'So?'

Oswald didn't answer, just scanned the overgrown yard outside, desperate for any sign of where they went. He wouldn't admit it, even to himself, but a small part of him hoped to see the corpses of Rinalta and Micah. At least then, he could take Aliya and leave this place without guilt. His soldier instincts were telling him to retreat, to regroup somewhere more defensible, to conserve his fighting power for a battle he could win. The thought of her disappointment wouldn't let him though.

Time to be more than a soldier.

He didn't know if it was his thought or not.

'No bodies,' he told Aliya. 'But I think there's another building out there, I can just make it out when the lightning flashes.'

'They could be hiding there.'

A feeling inside told him she was right. It was strange, to know something so surely and yet have no proof. Soldiers were a superstitious lot, trusting their guts in battle over logic at times. Oswald had never experienced the feeling though. He knew the others were in that building. He also knew it would be bad for him to go there.

'We need to help them,' Aliya practically pleaded.

How could a girl, an addict, who had obviously not had an easy life so quickly throw herself into danger to help strangers?

Turning, Oswald plucked the larger bits of glass from the frame, throwing them out into the yard. 'I'll help you out so you don't cut your feet,' he said, ignoring the feeling inside.

This girl thought he was some kind of hero. Maybe he was? 'Be careful climbing out.'

It was a tight fit for his bulky build, not to mention the fire lancing through his hands as he used them to haul himself through, but he got there with no small amount of grunted and swallowed curses. Turning back, he did his best to lower Aliya to the ground, trying to put her bare feet on the overgrown grass and avoid the shattered glass.

'Come on,' she said.

The cool rain had soaked him in an instant, making him cold all the way through, but at least the manor was blocking the majority of the wind. Wind was the real killer. He'd lost several green recruits to wind. 'Slow down,' he called, jogging to catch the girl. He thought she looked like a ghost, running through the rain in the tattered white dress. The cool rain soothed his burning hands, bringing him a minor measure of relief, however that only made his bad feeling about the building grow starker. His boots squelched on the water-soaked ground, the sound all but lost to the patter of the water hammering around him. Catching up to Aliya, he glanced around the yard, still amazed that they hadn't run into any darklings. It had sounded like the entire manor grounds had been riddled by them, and yet now there wasn't a single sign that they ever existed. Oswald gently pushed her behind him as they reached the building. It was little more than a garden shed.

Rain pattering on his head and the ground around him drowned out most sound, yet as they approached, he could make out something else, something that made his hackles rise.

It was Rinalta. 'Get off me!'

Panic. That was the sound of pure panic. He had heard it many times, and not just from raw recruits but also from veterans like himself. The feeling was a familiar one. He could hear scuffling and grunting. These were not the sounds of a darkling attack and yet he still recognised them; they were the sound of something far more evil to his mind.

The bad feeling almost overwhelmed him, every fibre of his being, every soldier instinct telling him to turn away.

Putting all his weight behind it, he raised his booted foot and shattered the door inwards off its hinges. It was dark inside, too dark to see anything in detail.

Oswald didn't need light.

He knew what was happening and where his enemy would be.

Reaching down, ignoring the fire in his hands, he grabbed a handful of grimy wool with each hand and yanked with all his strength. A body went flying backwards into the far wall, almost hitting Aliya as she stepped hesitantly into the shed behind him. It had been barely a split second since he had heard the sounds.

'I'm fine,' he heard Rinalta pant from the floor.

There was no thought. He had simply acted. Now, time and his awareness of the present seemed to wash back over him like a wave. Oswald turned towards the lithe figure he had just thrown against the wall.

Pain!

An icicle of pain shot through his chest, just below his sternum. He knew that pain. Had felt its cold embrace before. It wasn't the pain of a new injury. This was something else, something stark, something his bad feelings had tried to warn him against.

It was the cold pain of death.

His hands no longer burned. The ache in his back no longer mattered. There was no sharp stabbing in his knee anymore.

There was only the cold stab of ice in his chest.

'I'm sorry,' he heard a voice hiss in the dark. 'I'm so sorry… I…'

He didn't hear the rustle of a priest's robe fleeing into the storm.

Ice spread through him.

Thud.

Something hard was against his back now, but it didn't matter. A stunning figure of light appeared above him, looking down at him with ephemeral beauty.

He was glad she would be the last thing he saw.

Oswald closed his eyes.

The pain stopped at last.

The grass was warm and soft underneath him, almost welcoming him to slumber.

He lifted his head and blinked, eyes adjusting to the warm orange light all around him. Blinking twice, his eyes went wide as he pushed himself to his knees. For the first time in what felt like a lifetime, he didn't groan at the movement or cringe at the thought of being on his knees.

There was no pain.

The giant redwood tree was before him, only now it was larger, its green leaves glowing and bathing him in the orange light. There was no sun, just the light of the tree.

'Oswald,' the ephemeral voice called.

'Allmother,' he whispered, knowing she would hear him. This was her realm after all. Here, she was all. 'I did what I could. I tried...'

'I know.'

He turned and saw the familiar, glowing silhouette of a woman standing at the base of the gigantic tree, almost nestled in its roots. The smell of roses and wild berries washed over him. He felt warm. It wasn't heat, but rather a feeling; a feeling of love and contentment. He wanted nothing more than to lay down on the soft grass and sleep.

'The darklings,' he said instead. 'Rinalta, Aliya, they –'

'Peace, Oswald.' The glowing figure raised a hand. 'You have done exactly what you needed to do. You have protected the chosen one, given her the strength she will need to carry on. My other guardians will do the rest.'

A growl echoed from his left. Oswald turned to see the pale full moon rush towards him. Even here, in this place of peace and tranquillity, he felt fear and panic for the briefest of moments. The moon stopped in front of him. It was right there, close enough, he felt, that he could reach out and cup it in his hands. Instead, three shadows grew from it. The shadows resolved into snouts, elongating into the inky outlines of three massive wolves. They weren't exactly wolves; one had more of a fox shape to its head. Oswald could barely make out their features, but one thing was certain; these creatures were powerful.

Memory hit him. It was an old memory, almost completely lost to the years. His mother sat in her rickety old chair by the small fireplace in their cottage, telling him and his sisters of the protectors of men. 'The Allmother's Guardians.'

'Yes. Now rest.'

Oswald lay down again and closed his eyes. Sleep came quickly without the constant pang of pain.

13

Vengeance

Rinalta looked down at the shadow which had been Oswald, knowing she should reach out to the distraught Aliya, her body wracked with sobs as she knelt beside him. The door of the shack banged in its frame, wind blowing it open and closed as the storm tried to force its way into this tiny refuge. Aliya sobbed, face buried in the shirt of a man she had just met. Rinalta looked down at her and felt guilt. Guilt, because all she could feel was thankful that the soldier had stopped Micah's assault of her before he could do anything.

Her cheeks flushed in the dark. A molten weight burned in her heart, hotter than even her lust for vengeance against the traitor, Claudius, who had murdered her master.

Aliya sobbed though. Aliya sobbed and Rinalta felt helpless. Twice in one night, she had now felt like her power had left her. Twice she had been like a babe, unable to care for herself.

The molten core of anger grew hotter in her breast.

'I'm going after him,' she hissed, taking a step towards the door.

The claw like hand grabbing her wrist stopped her. She was surprised by the strength in the seraphim addict's grip. 'I'm coming with you,' Aliya said, sending a shiver down Rinalta's spine. Where she felt fire inside her, Aliya's voice was all ice, emotionless, deadly.

Rinalta bobbed her head in the dark. 'Let's go.'

The sound made her pause as she took another step. It was the sound of a blade being pulled from flesh; a sickly squelching sound. Rinalta did her best to not look at the flash of blade gripped in the girl's hand, but found her eyes drawn to it regardless.

'Stay quiet and stay behind me,' Rinalta said. She braced herself and then stepped back out into the downpour, crack of thunder and lightning splitting the sky as she did. Within a moment she was soaked through yet again, clothes sticking to her body. A shiver went down her spine that had nothing to do with the cold or wet.

Letting the mana build within her, she made the configuration for a basic detection spell, one that would show her the path Micah had fled on. Her mana reserves were dangerously low, but this particular spell took little, and she needed some way to follow him. Feeling the power respond to her wishes restored a level of calm she had not known she'd lost. Knowing the power still responded to her, knowing she was not powerless or helpless felt like a weight had been removed from atop her chest, letting her breathe again.

'Which way?' Aliya asked. Rinalta started. The girl looked like a woman in white, standing beside her in the dark, emaciated arms poking out from the tattered shift.

Focusing on the aqua ley lines her spell had created, Rinalta pointed. 'Into the forest.'

'What happened to the darklings?'

'I don't know.'

'They chased me and Oswald into the cellar, then left,' Aliya said, padding along beside her in the mud as they stepped into the trees yet again.

'They did the same to us. Something about this isn't right.'

'I know, they could have easily broken in and killed us.' Aliya's voice was still frozen, emotionless. Rinalta wasn't entirely sure how the young woman was still mobile; surely she was freezing and beyond terrified.

'Yes, but that's not what I mean,' Rinalta said. The canopy of the forest made the oppressive dark even worse, but it also provided a small amount of shelter from the storm, lessening the pounding of the rain and snap of thunder overhead. Rinalta was navigating mostly by instinct now, following the ley line through the pitch black. Despite this, Aliya was having no trouble keeping up. 'The whole situation is wrong. The four of us meeting in the house, Claudius showing up, the darklings; everything is wrong. There are far too many coincidences for this to be random chance.'

She could hear Aliya's feet squelching in the mud behind her, an echo of her own footfalls. Try as she might, Rinalta could find no way to stop the noise. She had always preferred cities to the countryside, a preference that had been reinforced by recent experience. Her only hope was that the sounds the two of them made were lost among the rumble of the storm and patter of rainfall. Time lost meaning in the darkness as the two women stalked their prey. How the priest had managed to find his way through the forest amid a storm was beyond Rinalta. He had not struck her as the hardy type. In fact, before the incident in the little shed, she would have described him as harmless. She shivered and made a mental note to be suspicious of the seemingly harmless from now on.

'What's that?' Aliya hissed, making Rinalta jump.

Thankful that the dark would have covered her fright, she squinted and looked through a gap in the trees, Aliya's pointed arm a blur of different coloured blackness next to her head. It had never occurred to her before tonight that there could be variations of darkness.

'Looks like a light, but it's too steady to be a fire,' Rinalta said, straining her eyes. 'He went straight towards it though, so that's where we are going too.' She couldn't bring herself to say his name. The mere thought of him made her feel unclean, like she had been coated with an invisible oil, doused and ready to be burned.

She stepped with greater care now, doing what she could to stop the squelching sound her boots made in the mud.

Aliya stuck close behind her. Rinalta wouldn't admit it, but she was thankful for the comforting presence of the skinny woman. As they approached the unnatural light, it was the radiance of power that told her what was making the light long before she could see it. The power had a warmth to it, but also a sour note, discordant in a way that was subtle and yet you knew was completely wrong. Her own power was like a warm spring day in a meadow of flowers. Inviting, comfortable, a delight to the senses. This power was the coming of a storm, still over the horizon yet marching inevitably towards the meadow. There was only one person out here who could generate this kind of power.

Claudius.

Hunching over, Rinalta and Aliya pushed through the sparse scrub and clawing branches of the trees. Rain still pounding around them, Rinalta thought they were being quite stealthy, even going so far as to congratulate herself silently for sneaking up on the traitor. Stopping behind a small bush, she peered through the leaves. Blinking a little from the glowing orange light, she could see him standing in front of the orb of power creating the light. A bubble emanated from the orb, encompassing the opening in the trees and stopping the rain like a force field. It was a simple configuration, but one that was impressive to those who were uninitiated in the ways of mana. Kneeling in the dirt before Claudius was the priest, head bowed.

'I can feel you out there, Rinalta,' called Claudius, eyes flickering towards the trees. 'You may as well come out.'

She cursed silently. Of course he would have felt her approach, regardless of how silent she had moved through the forest. 'Stay here,' she whispered to Aliya. 'Wait for an opportunity.'

The young woman nodded her understanding. Rinalta could only hope that Claudius had been so fixated on her mana signature, that he missed the flickering power within the addict.

'There she is,' Claudius said, arms spread wide as Rinalta stepped through the brush and into the light. 'Resplendent as always.'

His self-satisfied smile had anger boiling inside her, threatening to overwhelm common sense with the desire to start flinging as many fireballs as she could. He was far stronger than her though. She could feel his mana reserve radiating through the power of the light orb. Her own reserve was barely a flickering candle in comparison; the tumultuous events of the night having sapped her almost to breaking point.

Calm yourself, she thought. *Need to think strategically. I can't overpower him, so I need to outsmart him.* Rinalta took calm, measured steps. She needed more time to think but didn't want to look hesitant or weak.

'I understand our godly friend here tried to take advantage of you.' Claudius smirked, hand waving at the priest kneeling before him. The comment stunned her and she had to take a shuffling step to avoid falling on her face. She was trying to ignore Micah, who hadn't moved, and focus on the traitor first. Hopefully Aliya would deal with her would-be rapist and Rinalta could just go on ignoring him.

'Why did you do it?' Rinalta asked, voice loud and strong despite feeling as weak as a babe.

Claudius sighed. 'Still hung up on the death of your precious master.' He shook his head. 'I had hoped that leaving the cloistered life forced on you by the College of Rel would open your eyes.'

'Open my eyes?' Rinalta scoffed, pouring all the scorn she felt into her words. 'You're a traitor and a murderer, that's what my eyes are open to now.'

'Do you not see the extent of our power? Do you not see the things we could accomplish if unshackled from the dogmatic precepts of the college?'

Micah whimpered at his feet, drawing his attention away from her. It wasn't much, yet Rinalta acted, letting instinct take over as the configuration sprung alive. In a split second, she had a fireball in hand, burning with all the rage and fury she could pour into it, her mana pool emptying itself. It crossed the ten paces left between them, leaving a visible heatwave in its wake. Rinalta watched, helpless to do more as the fireball exploded in a gout of flame that, for a second, blotted out the orb of light. And for that second, Rinalta thought she might actually have succeeded.

But the light from the orb of power was still as consistent as ever, the orange glow still lighting the dark meadow, blocking out the rain.

As the smoke cleared, chains of power whipped towards her, wrapping around her twice and binding her in place. Her hands were caught at her sides, the power squeezing her, making it hard to breathe. And all she could hear was Claudius laughing. It pierced her soul, brought home her failure. It told her that no matter how powerful she thought she had been, it had never been enough.

She had failed, and now she was at the mercy of the traitor who had murdered her master.

Claudius stepped towards her, smile wide. 'Come Micah,' he said, gesturing for the priest to rise from where he had knelt throughout the entire confrontation. 'Let us see what kind of fun we can have.'

14

Lust

'Allmother guide and protect me from evil. Show me the path of righteousness. Forgive my wickedness and lead me into your loving embrace in the eternal afterlife.'

Micah didn't know if any god was listening, and yet a lifetime of dogmatic belief left him with the need to pray, even if only to assuage his own guilty conscience. The mud seeped through the rags which his vestment had devolved into. It was cold, wet, sticky, altogether horrible, and yet he barely noticed. Now, in his darkest moment, he finally found a modicum of peace in prayer such as the other adherents of Laran would always speak of.

A barking laugh broke his peace. The cold seeped back into both his body and heart.

'You mutter and pray to the Allmother yet recite a prayer from the holy book of Laran. Even if either had any true power, they would not listen to your pathetic whimpering.' Claudius looked down at him, bathed in the heretical orange glow that lit the glade, its bubble keeping the omnipresent rain at bay.

Another shiver passed through him. The harsh and stark memory of what he had done in the shed burned his heart with shame. But even the shame and guilt could not supress the yearning he felt at the memory of Rinalta's body pressed up against his own. He had come so close to finally satisfying the craving. Almost, he had succumbed to the lust. Even his vile sin, the pain he had caused to Oswald after that could not diminish the memory of her flesh.

'What have either of these gods ever done for you, except torment you,' Claudius continued, oblivious to his inner turmoil. 'I can see your pain and struggles. I can see your deepest desire and how you have been forced by your cruel god to supress them. Your so-called merciful and just god has forbidden you one of the sweetest of pleasures that a man can taste. Why pray to him? Why now pray to the Allmother who would shackle you just as tightly?'

The man's words washed over and through him, resonating with his soul, uncaging the rage that had laid hidden deep inside his breast for years. A heat washed through him, and this time it was not lust. For so long, he had prayed. For so long he had genuflected at the altar of Laran, and now he knelt in the mud praying to the Allmother. And what had that gotten him? He had suppressed his urges, denied himself the pleasure of the flesh, admonishing those who indulged in it while secretly craving it. Twice now, his passion had led him to attack innocent women, and twice he had been stopped before culmination. Why? Why would a merciful and loving god, one whom he devoted his life to, curse him with such urges? It didn't make sense.

'That's right,' Claudius said. His face was lit with the orange glow, one side in shadow, a toothy grin staring down at him. 'They have been torturing you for years, denying you sweet release. And for what? What reward have you reaped?'

Claudius's words stuck in his head. They stoked the fire in his breast.

'You should not be denying yourself. You are a man and deserve to indulge in your senses, you deserve to satisfy the cravings of your flesh. Your gods have denied you this, but my God... he can set you free from inhibition, set you free from the shackles on your body and soul.'

Micah was in a trance. All his years of pious dedication were a sham. A cruel trick to make him torture himself for the pleasure of harsh and unforgiving gods. Claudius spoke, a stream of words, a litany of a new faith that promised to provide him the relief that he deserved and had been withheld from him for so long now. A new prayer came forth from his lips. A new prayer that the priest in ragged robes took up with a fervour that had previously escaped him through his life of worship.

He was still kneeling before Claudius when she stepped into the orange dome. Micah noticed because Claudius's words ceased; but his own prayers continued unabated. At least, until the memory resurfaced. He thought of Yesmina, who had first stirred his lust to breaking point, an event that now seemed a lifetime ago. Then the memory of Rinalta squirming under him in the woodshed. His desire flared and a needful moan escaped his bloodless lips. The priest was pulled back to the present as a burst of heat washed over him, Claudius disappearing momentarily in a puff of fire on his peripheral. Micah didn't worry though. There was no way his new god would let a powerful acolyte like Claudius perish; or at least, not before he taught Micah of his new god's ways. He could almost feel the web of fate hanging over him, embracing him, setting him on the correct path.

The smoke cleared and Micah looked up at Claudius who was casually brushing non-existent dust from the front of his embroidered jacket. *How has he kept it clean and dry?* he couldn't help wondering.

Claudius looked at him. 'Come Micah,' he said, gesturing for him to rise. 'Let us see what kind of fun we can have.'

The tattered priest rose. No cold slowed him, his joints moved freely, standing with an ease that spoke of his unburdening. There was nothing weighing him down now. His eyes drank in Rinalta as she slumped to her knees, exhaustion finally overwhelming her. At their first meeting, Micah had been sure she was an angel, sent to deliver him from his burdens, a being of sublime beauty, a Valkyr of legend. His eyes were open now though. He now knew that she was not a deliverer, but rather a temptress that had been sent by his former cruel gods to further his torment.

Dogmatic belief fell away from him like a suit of armour, clanking to the ground around him, allowing him to move without constraint for the first time in his life. He looked at the woman, now kneeling before him, tired eyes shining up at him in the orange glow of the dome. Micah knew what his new god wanted. Micah knew that she was his gift now. She had been delivered to him, changed from temptress into his sweet release. It was time for him to unleash the full weight of his lust, to finally have succour. The priest stepped forward, still dressed in tattered rags, splattered with mud, but now invested with a strength born of holy zeal. Claudius stepped with him and they loomed over Rinalta.

'Give in to the temptation Micah. Sate your thirst upon her.' Claudius raised a hand, ever so slightly, gesturing him forward towards Rinalta.

Micah took one step forward and stopped. Tears tracks stained her face, washing away dirt that even the heavy rain beyond the orange dome had failed to clean. A wave of disgust roiled in his gut. At first, he thought it was disgust at himself, for what he was about to do. Then the new litany that Claudius had taught him revealed the truth. He was disgusted at her, disgusted that she would cry right before he blessed her, disgusted that she would so disdain the holy gift he intended to deliver unto her.

It is time.

The thought whisked through his head. The tattered priest wasn't sure it was even his thought, but that didn't matter anymore. Rinalta jerked, raising a hand at them.

He was about to step back, expecting another magical blow to come, when the laughter booming from Claudius stopped him. Waving his hand languidly, an invisible force hit Rinalta, sending her lurching backwards into the mud, limbs sprawling as she fell. Her ivory face was stunned, flawless skin splattered with mud, her once bright eyes now foggy and dazed as she tried to recover from the blow.

'She's waiting for you,' Claudius said. There was something predatory to his smile. Something feral.

Micah didn't care. Rinalta lay waiting for him.

He knelt between her legs, one hand clasping harshly on her thigh, forcing her knees apart. The tattered priest's blood was boiling, desire washing through him in furious waves, stoked to a fury as he savoured the experience, making sure he took in every carnal sense, relishing the feel of her muscle in his grip, the way her raven hair haloed around her face. He reached down, ready to disrobe her, to open his gift. Unlike his aborted attempt in the shed, she could not fight him this time. The blow Claudius had struck was clearly more than a physical strike. It was as if Rinalta was in a trance, aware but unable to command her body to act against him. Micah breathed the litany, his new prayer, the prayer to a god that would finally reward him for his unwavering faith and devotion. Hand still gripping her thigh, pushing her legs apart, he reached down with his other hand and clasped the top of her trousers.

The scream stopped him after a single yank at her pants. She still lay motionless, staring up at him from the mud, disgust, disdain, and fear all written clearly in her watery blue eyes. It hadn't been her that screamed.

Everything seemed to be happening at once. Releasing his grip on Rinalta's pants, Micah turned just in time to see a spectre launching itself behind Claudius, landing on his back as it let out the hideous shriek again.

Claudius bellowed as an arc of red splattered through the air. Spinning with inhuman speed, his shout still echoing under the orange dome, he flung the white form from his back, sending it rolling to a stop before the priest.

'Aliya,' Micah muttered, recognising the seraphim addict. He had forgotten about her in his fervour and now turned surprised eyes towards Claudius.

A knife protruded from his shoulder blade. It was a soldier's dagger, utilitarian but deadly in the right hands. Or in incompetent but lucky hands like his own when he had used it to stab Oswald. He had known, as soon as the blade had slid into the man, that it had been a killing blow. Seeing the blade, watching as Claudius used his arcane power to withdraw it from his flesh with an invisible hand, brought that moment flooding back to him, along with the horror that he had ended a man's life.

Aliya moaned in the mud before him, rolling over to her hands and knees.

Claudius groaned, eyes closing as the tip of the blade finally slid free of his flesh.

Micah felt numb for just a moment. That moment was enough.

A blow struck the side of his head, pain and dizziness overwhelming him. His face hitting the wet mud was a distant sensation, noticeable at first only from the way it made the pain in his head surge like lightning. More screams reached him, followed by several booms that felt like they were shaking the very earth underneath him. It felt like a lifetime, a lifetime of his thoughts trudging through a mud pit of pain and nausea, but was barely a few seconds, before his wits started to return. He levered himself up onto his knees.

Rinalta was on her feet, now at the far side of the dome, locked in yet another magical battle with Claudius. Micah didn't worry. Claudius clearly had the upper hand despite his fresh wound, batting away the motes of power she flung at him almost contemptuously.

Fighting down the urge to vomit, blinking deliberately as he forced his vision to focus, Micah managed to fight his way to his feet. He hoped Claudius didn't do too much damage to Rinalta; she was his gift after all, and he had yet to satisfy his yearnings. A flush of heat at how close he had once again been helped clear his mind, bringing purpose to his body once again. He glanced at the battle for just a moment, before the flutter of white drew his attention away.

Aliya, in her dirty white dress - more a shift really - was charging towards him, knife gripped in trembling fist, deadly purpose written across her emaciated face. His heart thump. Panic welled up. He was a priest, not a fighter, and his first instinct was to run from the danger.

She gave him no chance to.

Slashing out, she swung the blade in a wild arc at his stomach. His knees buckled as he tried to lurch back out of range from the blow that would surely disembowel him. His body dropped before his jelly legs were able to catch him, the knife slicing a shallow ribbon across his chest. Sharp pain flared where the knife bit and he could feel the welling of blood before it began to trickle down his chest, his manky vestment sticking to it. A flash of steel warned him. Aliya was following her first strike with a backswing, the full weight of her stick-like body behind it, face twisted into a hateful snarl. His knees buckled again, gut clenching, the shimmer of death rushing towards his throat in the form of a steel blade. Instead, he stumbled forward, legs struggling to catch him this time, sending him inside the arc of the blade to crash into Aliya with his shoulder.

They went down in a tangle of limbs. Another shot of pain lanced through him, his forehead cracking against Aliya's as they splattered into the mud. Dazed, he tried to push himself up but had to turn and vomit as the dizziness threaten to overwhelm him. A groan reached him. Something squirmed underneath him and for a moment he thought the very ground was trying to swallow him. He blinked, realising he was on Aliya, knocked senseless by their fall and stuck underneath his body.

Micah looked around, searching for Claudius and Rinalta. The orange bathed glade was silent, the sound of crackling and booming magic finally silenced. He saw Rinalta, bent over and panting before Claudius who stood erect, unflappable in his superiority.

'What about the darklings?' Rinalta's voice reached him. She could barely form the words around her breathless pants.

Claudius barked a laugh. 'They are mine to command, a gift from my new god and soon to be lord of this world. I used them to funnel you all here.'

'But why?' Rinalta tried to straighten. A grimace of pain flashed across her face as she bent double, retching and clasping her stomach with both arms.

'For the entertainment, mostly. But also to counter the Allmother's influence.'

Aliya groaned under him again, her shifting body rubbing up against him as he lay on her, propped up by a single arm. He was curious about the darklings and the part they were playing in his new gods plan, but Claudius could enlighten him another time. He looked down at the addict laying beneath him. She was far from the sumptuous meal that Rinalta represented, but there was a certain attractiveness, even if she was all bones. Micah's blood heated and his body responded. He wanted Rinalta, wanted her deliciously curved form, wanted to take his time with her, but his body, so long denied, pressed irresistible urges upon him.

Why not a little appetiser before the main meal. The thought crossed his mind, at once his own thought and yet somehow not.

His body responded.

Wrenching up Aliya's dress, which was just as tattered and stained as his own robes, he took in the sight of that which had been so long denied to him. It was both the most amazing, glorious thing he had seen, and yet somehow also anticlimactic. He pulled up his robe and grasped himself, groaning at the pleasure of his own touch, at the anticipation of how much better it was about to feel. Pressing himself down, he placed his tip against her. She was moist and warm. He groaned. Climax built up and he spilt his seed on her. The release was euphoric and yet he knew greater pleasure still awaited him, his fire still burning, his body still hard with desire. It took several fumbling attempts, his own eagerness getting in his way.

But finally, he managed to position himself right, crying out as he slid inside of her, feeling a pleasure beyond anything he could have imagined while pleasuring himself in the solitude of his monastery cell. Closing his eyes, willing himself to not climax again so soon, he reached up and clenched a hand on her almost non-existent breast, gripping it harshly, feeling the hard nipple under his thumb and twisting it. He pumped as he did so, unable to stop himself, and felt his seed spill inside her.

He groaned and cried, then opened his eyes to look down at Aliya.

Her eyes were open.

There was a flash of steel and then agony. A bolt of lightning shot through his eye as the blade pierced it and darkness descended.

Micah awoke.

He couldn't move.

At first he thought the Allmother had summoned him once again to the world between worlds where her tree of life sheltered all. But there was no sense of peace here.

Pain flared at his wrists and ankles. Cold iron bit into his skin cruelly, the shackles holding him firm against a vertical rack, his body dangling from them. He blinked. Pain bloomed in his right eye.

The Dagger! he thought. Pain bit his wrists again as he tried in vain to reach for his eye where he knew the dagger would still be. He blinked tears from his one working eye and tried to figure out where he was.

It was dark. Fires burned in the distance, the kind that lit the sky across the entire horizon. As far as he could tell, he was suspended on some sort of raised stone dais, looking down on a jagged black plain of harsh obsidian. The euphoria he had felt at finally satisfying his dark urges was gone. As he thought about what he had done to Aliya, his blood heated and his body responded once again.

'That's right,' an ephemeral voice boomed. It was deep and harsh, the voice of menace incarnate, and Micah knew he was hearing the voice of his new god. 'Your lust has not been satisfied, and now that you have failed me, it never will be, little priest.'

Three figures appeared, stepping from the shadows around the dais. As they stepped close to him, their shapes resolved into that of three beautiful women. But Micah thought beautiful did not do them justice. They were beauty made flesh, each with a figure made to be held, and yet each slightly different in build. There was a blonde, a brunette, and a red head. All were naked. His lust surged to heights he had never experience before, looking down on these paragons of beauty and loveliness, imagining what it would be like to have just one of them in his embrace.

'This would have been your reward,' his god said.

Micah couldn't help the groan that escaped him as pain and lust both flared. He knew what was coming.

'And now, they will be your eternal torment.'

The women started touching each other, started pleasuring each other, moaning and writhing as they lived out his every fantasy before him. He was helpless. All he could do was watch and suffer.

He knew this torment would never end. Pain shot through his wrists and ankles; a lightning bolt arced in the eye with the protruding dagger. His pain mixed with his desire in an unholy coupling of torment.

The tattered priest knew he was damned. The tattered priest knew he had chosen the wrong god.

15

Retribution

Warm blood gushed over her hand, dripping down onto her breasts as the priest went limp. With a heave, Aliya rolled him sideways. She put as much contempt into the shove as she could muster, body heaving with half-sobs, the disgust barely noticeable as it was wreathed with rage.

She had been used before. She had been a seraphim addict after all. She had allowed unspeakable things to be done to her simply for a hit of the drug.

And yet, she had never been enraged like this before. Choice. Her tired mind decided it came down to choice. Every time before, it had been her choice to be used. This time, the foul zealot had decided it was his right to use her body.

Well, she had proved him wrong. He would never take that liberty with another woman again. Not only that, Oswald, the hulking bear of a man who had shown her such gentleness had been avenged. She had barely known the soldier, yet still she felt a warmness inside as she thought of him, a warmness she could only describe as love.

Rolling to her side in the mud, Aliya tugged down the tattered remnants of her dress. Her underwear was beyond retrieval, half buried in the slick, cold earth underneath Micah's cooling body, his already pale face now ashen, his features contorted into a look of shock.

A cruel laugh drew her attention.

Across the dome, lit by the ethereal orange glow, stood Claudius, the rogue mage. Rinalta knelt before him. With a casual wave, he sent Rinalta sprawling sideways, sliding through the mud towards where Aliya was climbing to her feet. Aliya had not been able to see the magical blow but the force of it was unmistakable. For a moment Aliya was certain Rinalta was dead. And yet, defying all logic, Rinalta stirred, a breathless groan escaping her lips.

Standing, Aliya stalked forwards. She had only met Rinalta that night, and yet she knew there was a bond between them. Micah was dead, the vengeance she had sought now carried out, but she had no thoughts of fleeing and saving herself. Claudius watched her approach, crooked grin on his chiselled face even as he glanced at Micah's corpse.

'A shame,' he said. 'That one had such promise to my master. His well of depravity was deeper than most, a life of repression digging his already perverted well of darkness even deeper. It is often those who profess to be the most holy, the purest, who fall into darkness.' He looked towards Aliya as if expecting her to understand.

Aliya had reached Rinalta and knelt to grip her arm. 'Are you alright.'

Rinalta groaned, but with Aliya's help, manage to sit upright. Blood was oozing from her nose and ears.

'We need to get out of here,' Aliya whispered. She may have killed Micah, but she had no delusions that she could even hope to injure the corrupt mage. Her eyes flicked to the tree line, just beyond the orange glow of the dome, trying to calculate how quick she could get to it while helping Rinalta. Without seraphim though, she was stuck with reality, and the reality was her body's strength had been wasted away from years of drug abuse. She knew she would be lucky to make it alone, let alone helping another woman, before being struck down with a fireball or bolt of lightning.

'It's no use,' Claudius said. He stood, ten paces away, watching with a tilted head as she tried to haul Rinalta to her feet. 'You cannot escape. Even if you somehow defeat me and make it into the forest, my darklings will tear you to shreds before you can make it a league.'

'Why are you doing this?' The question fell from Aliya before she realised she was going to ask it.

'Why should I tell you?'

'You're going to kill us anyway, why not tell us?' She managed to get Rinalta to a standing position, arm draped over her shoulders as her emaciated form took most of the woman's weight.

'Clever,' Claudius said with a smile. 'But no, I'm not going to tell you. I am a servant of my master's will. His plans and reasons are not mine to share, even to the dead.'

'But the darklings,' Aliya groaned, Rinalta's weight already bearing her down.

'Pawns. Lesser servants. Nothing more. Hardly more than foot soldiers in the grand scheme of things.'

Keep him talking, she thought to herself. 'Not like you.'

Another crooked smirk. 'I see why she chose you. Much smarter than a simple seraphim addict. Enough idle chatter though, it's time to be done with this.' Claudius waved his hand.

The blow of force knocked the wind from her lungs first, then sent her tumbling backwards, her arms and legs tangling with Rinalta's as they fell. Rinalta's weight pinned her in the mud. Aliya was face up, looking at the roof of the orange dome above them, whereas Rinalta had somehow spun around in mid-air and was now face down, head next to Aliya's right shoulder. Managing to gasp in air after a moment, Aliya tried to roll Rinalta off her. In the distance, a howl of wolves echoed through the night, reaching them through the trees. *The darklings will kill them,* she thought sadly to herself, thinking of the majestic beasts.

Rinalta's hand grasped tight on her bicep as they clambered to their feet together. 'Get ready to run,' she whispered.

Aliya looked her in the eye. A familiar look greeted her. One of acceptance. One of fate.

The pain from yet another force blow from Claudius registered dully in her mind. Physical pain was a distant nuisance. It was the absence of mana that was burning her through. Only once during her training had she been so drained of the wondrous energy that made up the universe.

'You must know where the limits of your power are, Rinalta,' Master Gerard had told her, pacing around her on the crushed stone of the practice yard. 'You must understand what it feels like to be drained of mana, to understand why you should never push yourself to the extreme. Now, configure another fireball spell.'

She had protested. The configuration had felt like trying to wrangle wet noodles with those annoying little eating sticks her master often forced her to eat with. Master Gerard had not cared for her complaints. Another fireball configuration had snapped to life in her hands.

Fighting Claudius had left her empty. Hollowed out. A husk of the person she had been.

And yet, despite the pit inside her, despite everything in her head telling her to give up, to surrender to the black abyss of death, her body kept going.

Rinalta had thought herself alone. She had been sure Aliya had been killed by Micah, and yet, defying her wildest expectations, the stick of a girl had returned to try to help her. *Idiot,* she thought to herself. *She should have run while she had the chance.* Even if they had somehow stopped Claudius, there were still the darklings in the forest to deal with. She felt her body shift, felt the groan escape from her chapped lips as Aliya pushed her.

Her mind being so completely divorced from her body was not a good thing. She knew this. She didn't care. But still she wondered at the seraphim addict. What kept her going? What kept her fighting? Surely, she had less to live for than Rinalta, and yet Rinalta had all but given up. Using what little physical energy she had left, Rinalta tilted her head as the girl tried to move her and looked into her blue eyes.

Life.

She saw life in the addict's eyes. Aliya may have been dealt a shitty hand in life, but she was still fighting for it, fighting to go on, fighting for the hope that things will get better.

Something deep inside Rinalta, deeper than the well of mana that was now empty, stirred.

Master Gerard's words reached through time for her again. 'It is when we are at our worst, at our weakest, that we discover who we truly are.'

She hadn't known what he meant at the time. He had told her that the words will make sense when they needed to make sense. His cryptic lessons had always pissed her off; not that she told him that though. As always though, he had proven correct. Rinalta finally understood. The howl of wolves pulled her attention back to the present.

Mustering her strength, ignoring the pain that coursed through her body as she allowed her mind to reconnect to it fully, Rinalta gripped Aliya's bicep. 'Get ready to run.'

Aliya nodded, then helped her fully to her feet.

Claudius smirked at them. She could feel him focusing his mana into a configuration, recognised it as a blade of air. He was going to finish them off. Rinalta smirked back.

'Run,' she hissed at Aliya, pushing the girl away. Thankfully, the little seraphim addict didn't hesitate.

The blade of air shot out from Claudius's hand. Rinalta could see the displacement as it arced towards her, feel the power behind it. She held up her hand, energy shield crackling to life just before it struck, dissipating the blade of air as easily as a cliff stopped the waves. But like the cliff, standing strong, it still chipped away at her.

'You fool!' Claudius snarled. His smirk was gone, instead replaced with anger that barely concealed his fear. She could see it in the way blood drained from his face in the orange glow and the hair that lifted on the nape of his neck. Her senses had snapped to a razor sharpness, one that even the power could not replicate. 'You would kill us both.'

'Yes.'

Time slowed as she drew the power.

It wasn't mana. No. Her mana was gone. She reached beyond that empty pit, reached deeper into herself and tapped a forbidden power.

She tapped her own life force.

It was golden.

It was glorious.

It was powerful.

She looked at Claudius who moved as if stuck in molasses. Distantly, his shrill shriek reached her.

Not vengeance, she thought to herself. *Retribution!*

Her anger seeped away as she let go of her power, letting it burst from her body.

~

Aliya ran.

Her breath was already coming in ragged pants, her legs leaden as she pushed them for more speed which they could not muster. Seraphim addiction had robbed her body of its vitality, and the events of the night had left what little physical energy she had exhausted.

Still, she ran.

It felt like bare seconds when she heard Claudius shriek. Goosebumps prickled her flesh at the sound.

A wave of force hit her back, launching her forward into the air. Her arms pinwheeled as she flew, mind frantic as it tried to adjust to her new spinning reality. Almost unconsciously, she noticed the orange glow that had filled the glade had disappeared in an instant. She was still in the air when the pelting rain hit her cold body again. A flash of white streaked between the trees as she fell, the howl of wolves louder now.

Breath rushed from her lungs as she hit the soggy ground. Pain lanced through her as she gasped, black flecks flickering across her vision as it dimmed and she passed out once again.

~

Rinalta floated in darkness.

The pain, emptiness, and anger were gone. She felt... free.

She knew she was dead. Knew that channelling her life force had caused an explosion which had torn her apart, reducing her physical body to dust. And she also knew that Claudius could not have escaped the blast alive.

Vengeance was hers.

No! Not vengeance. Retribution. His death had been nothing greater than he had deserved.

The darkness lifted, replaced with a warm orange glow. At first, she thought she was back in the glade, that Claudius was still alive in his dome. But this was a different glow. It was as if the dome had been a poor parody of the power that now surrounded her, embraced her like a mother cradling a child, or a lover holding her in the night. It was warm and comforting. She felt herself move. Rinalta didn't know when or how it had happened, but she once again had form.

Taking a step, a great redwood tree loomed above her, appearing as if from a mist. Soft grass massaged her bare feet, the scent of roses filling the air around her. The urge to lay under that tree and sleep was almost overwhelming.

'You have done well, Rinalta.'

She jumped, newly formed head swivelling, although she could not see where the ephemeral voice had come from.

'Who are you?' She asked with a shaky voice, although she felt no fear.

'You have protected my chosen one. You let go of your anger and sacrificed yourself for her.'

'Allmother?' Her memory stirred and she thought of the other three speaking to her of the ancient god as they had sat in the dilapidated house together. She had scoffed at the time.

'I could not reach you earlier, not while you were wrapped in etherium, the power that you call mana.'

Her head spun, trying to put the pieces together. 'Aliya is your chosen? A seraphim addict?' She couldn't help the laugh that escaped.

'No. Not her, although she is a crucial part, just as Oswald was.'

Rinalta laughed. It wasn't her normal sarcastic laugh. This was a laugh of pure joy.

'Rest now, protector,' the Allmother said.

Rinalta lay on the soft grass and closed her eyes, content in the knowledge that she had completed her task.

~

Pain.

Pain lanced through Aliya's entire being.

Pain like she had never felt before. Worse even than the pain she had endured that fateful night in the forest nine months earlier when the wolves had howled and the shadows feared.

'That's it darling,' Helga said, her normally booming voice now gentle. 'One more push.'

Aliya pushed.

The pain was excruciating. The pain was worth it.

She was rewarded with a high-pitched wail; a scream of life that touched her heart and made it skip a beat.

'A daughter,' Helga said.

She blinked tears from her eyes and took her daughter in her arms, revelling in the feel of her warm little body as she lay on her chest.

'What will you name her?' One of Helga's apprentices asked from her bedside.

A boom sounded from outside, drawing their attention for a moment, followed by men shouting and the clink of steel.

'Damn darklings are pushing hard tonight,' Helga muttered, washing her hands in a basin. 'Never you mind though, deary, the Allmother shields this bastion and the brave soldiers who protect us.'

Aliya smiled, looking down at her daughter who looked back with the eyes of the man that had defended her from the darkness. She could see Oswald so clearly in her. Could practically feel him in the room with them.

A pack of wolves howled outside. She knew there were three out there, watching over her small house in the darkness. Three wolves that were not wolves.

'Her name?'

Aliya stroked her daughters little tuft of black hair and answered. 'Retribution.'

16

Duty

Septimus sighed and heaved himself to his feet again as the line crept forward. One of the wheels of the wagon in front of him screeched horribly and he was certain it was about to fall off its axle. But still it plodded forward, moving with the press of people just like him.

'No weapons allowed,' someone ahead shouted.

The fort walls loomed before him, hard faced men looking down at the rabble, spears and bows ready for use at a moments notice. Fort Astral was already becoming famous. It had held against the darkling scourge as all others were overrun. It was now the last bastion of safety in the east and refugees were streaming from across the countryside to seek shelter behind the spiked logs that encircled it. Septimus had been here once before, many years ago when his master had first taken him to his tower.

His heart caught in his chest a moment. Almost a year later and still he grieved the passing of his master, Praetores, champion of the Weavers of Fate. Pushing it aside, he finally passed under the gate, nodding absently at the rules the guards were yelling.

Paying the squelching mud no mind, he slogged over to the side of the street, taking shelter under the eave of a small hut and letting the stream of refugees pass. Closing his eyes, he reached out. His senses expanded. Letting his mind free, it detached from his body, the link held only by a tether as he followed the pull of power. For a year he had followed that pull. Before that, it had always been close by, in the cave near the tower, the holy charge he had sworn to protect along with Master Praetores. Being this close to it again was almost like being home.

Almost.

Fort Astral was filled to bursting. The dense aura of humanity was almost enough to blot out his ability to find the power. But he hadn't come this far to fail.

'Hey, what you hanging round me house for?'

The scratchy voice pulled him back to his body. His head reeled from the sudden shift back to physicality, something he had always struggled with.

'Not looking to do some thieving I hope,' the old man shook a gnarled finger in his face. 'All yous refugees be looking to thieve something.'

'I'll be on my way,' Septimus said politely. He pulled his cloak around him and stepped back out into the mud of the street. The press had lessened; the crowd of refugees having been pushed deeper into the fort by the guards to they didn't crowd the gate. The old man barked a few curses after him, but Septimus ignored them. He knew where he was going now.

It took him almost an hour to reach the small hut, nestled behind the longhouse near the communal stable. The fort wasn't large, a small town really, but every street he had turned down had been thick with people, makeshift shelters slung between the permanent buildings everywhere. Annoyance filled him at the delay. He was so close. And yet, he pushed the feeling aside, proud that even in the darkest days, the Legionary of the Order of Light still held true to their ancient oaths to protect all who asked for it, to shelter rich and poor, healthy and sick, in the light of the Allmother. He knew their order had forgotten a lot of its history, his master had spent months making him learn it all, but the central tenets that bound the warriors together still held. They were the shield of the Allmother.

Glancing in the stables as he passed, he saw only a few sickly-looking mares. The living conditions within the fort were degrading fast and would only get worse as more refugees crowded inside and the darklings spread their influence across the land.

Halting, he stood before the hut; three large square stones marked a path to the thick front door. He had expected to be led to the longhouse. He had expected the one he was searching for to be living in a place of honour. Instead, he looked at a hut, thatched roof showing signs of disrepair, an ill-fitting shutter rattling in the window. Still, after seeing how many were living in the fort, having solid walls around you could be considered a luxury.

His boots left muddy tracks on the stone path as he stepped up to the door. He raised a hand to bang on it just as it was pulled open. Septimus froze, arm in the air, mouth agape as he looked on the woman before him.

She was beautiful.

Golden hair flowed down over her shoulders in waves, her slim figure filling the blue dress, pale blue eyes bright and full. His breath caught in his chest, and he could feel his cheeks flushing hot.

The woman raised an eyebrow at him. 'Can I help you?' Her voice was soft and singsong.

Septimus shut his mouth so fast he clacked his teeth together, sweat breaking out on his brow as his face flushed even more. 'I... um, that is... My name is Septimus.' He had always considered himself mature for his age, raised by the wise Praetores, but before this paragon of feminine beauty, he felt just like the seventeen-year-old that he was.

'Well Septimus, do you want to tell me why you were about to bang on my door?'

He didn't know what to say. For a year he had followed the power, for a year he had yearned for this moment, to carry out his duty, and yet he had never once considered what he would say once he found them.

A baby crying in the hut broke the silence between them. The woman glanced back over her shoulder, then back at Septimus, eyes roving over him carefully. 'You look like you could use something to eat.' Something seemed to soften inside her at the words. 'You can come in as long as you swear to the Allmother that you mean us no harm.'

Septimus blinked. 'Of course,' he stammered, 'I mean, I swear on the Allmother I mean you no harm. I –'

'Come in then,' she cut him off. As she stood to the side, beckoning him in, he saw her tuck a dagger back into a sheath on her belt. He hadn't noticed she was holding it but had no doubt she would have used it had he proven a danger.

'There's a bit of stew left in the pot, bowls on the table,' she said. 'Help yourself.' She stepped over to a small crib and lifted out a child, maybe four months old, but Septimus was no expert when it came to children. He couldn't even remember the last time he had been in a room with one. The woman sat on a rocking chair next to the fireplace and, without warning, undid her blouse and began to feed the child.

Swallowing a small cry, Septimus almost choked, blushing as he turned away from her and looked around the hut. It was small, a single room, with a fire along the far wall, a table in the middle and a bed pushed up against one wall, crib sitting next to it. There was nothing lavish about it, strictly utilitarian he thought, and yet the warmth and pleasant smell of flowers gave it a homely feel that his master's tower could never replicate. His master had always told him there was more magic in the world than the power of etherium. Septimus was starting to realise that and thought the power a woman had to turn a hut into a home was one of them.

'Help yourself,' the woman said again. 'Tribby will be asleep again soon, she is a greedy girl.' She said it with a small laugh and smile.

'Thank you,' he said and then hesitated, hand on a bowl. 'I'm sorry, I didn't get your name, mine is Septimus.' It all came out in a rush, and he felt like a bumbling fool, especially when he realised he had already introduced himself.

'It's nice to meet you Septimus. You can call me Aliya, and this is Tribby.'

'Tribby?'

'Short for Retribution,' Aliya explained, smiling down at her daughter who was already falling asleep at her breast.

Septimus let his senses extend outwards again and gasped, dropping the bowl back onto the table in his shock. 'It's her.'

'What's her?' Aliya asked, a tinge of suspicion in her voice. She pulled her now sleeping daughter away from her chest, completely unashamed as she bared herself while putting the baby back in her crib.

Septimus coughed and turned away. To distract himself, he picked up the bowl again and scooped some stew from the pot hanging over the banked coals, taking the sole seat at the table.

'You going to answer me? What's her?' Aliya stood, one hand on her dagger, looking down on Septimus across the table.

'She's the vessel,' Septimus blurted out, unsure how else to say it. All this way, all this time, and he had never thought about what he would say. *Master would be disappointed,* he rebuked himself.

'Vessel?'

'Yes, for the Allmother's power, her etherium. It was released from the well over a year ago. I've been following it's trace ever since; it's my duty to protect it.'

Her hand slipped from the dagger as she sat back in the rocking chair. 'Your duty? You seem a little young for that.'

'Well, it was my master's duty, you see. We are the Weavers of Fate, my master was the champion of the order.'

Aliya just shook her head. Septimus was surprised she had never heard of them.

'We serve the Allmother, have been protecting her well of power for centuries. A being of darkness attacked though.' He shivered at the memory of the figure in the mist, towering over his master as he stood on the cliff top. 'My master sacrificed himself so the power had time to escape. I knew it was likely looking for a host to inhabit after all this time, someone to become the embodiment of the Allmother on the mortal plane. I never expected this though.' He pointed at the crib. 'The Allmother's power has chosen your daughter.'

Septimus had been expecting shock from Aliya, but instead she sat calmly, eyes on Retribution's crib. He was on the verge of saying more when she nodded and spoke.

'That explains a lot,' she said softly. 'What will you do now?'

Again, he was at a loss. 'Protect her, I guess.' Aliya was looking at him intently. 'And you too,' he added in a rush.

She stared at him, not moving, not saying a word, just stared and studied. He took a bite of the stew, blowing on it before eating. A groan escaped him at the taste. After so long on the road, even a simple, warm meal like the venison and vegetable stew was ecstasy, hunger enhancing his sense of taste.

'I want to tell you about Retribution's father and how we met,' Aliya said. Septimus stopped, another spoon of stew half-way to his lips as she launched into her story. It was getting dark by the time she finished. Retribution had awoken throughout and spent much of the story being bounced on Aliya's knee as she spoke of the darkling's attack on Zailhiem and her former life as a seraphim addict. This had shocked Septimus, especially as she spoke of the emaciated wreck she had become. There was little evidence of that life now; she looked healthy and vibrant to the young man. She told him of the three other travelers she had met and the night of trials they had endured, trapped together in a dilapidated mansion as they were beset by darklings and a dark-mage. There was pain in her voice as she spoke of the soldier, Oswald. Septimus sat in rapt attention until the very end, when she told him of the wolves that had protected her as she escaped through the forest. He agreed with her when she said she believed them to be the fabled guardians of the Allmother. His stew was cold by the time she finished.

He sat in his chair, staring at both Aliya and Retribution, sitting happily together in the rocking chair.

Bells tolled in the distance. Aliya sat up straight, her now tired eyes coming alert.

'What does that mean?'

'Darklings,' she answered.

A wolf howled in the distance, just before the shouting began. Septimus and Aliya both stood, about to see what was happening outside when a heavy hand banged on the door.

'Aliya, girl, are you there?'

She clearly recognised the voice because she was moving on swift feet to the door, yanking it open, Retribution balanced on one hip.

'Helga, what's happening?'

'Darklings, lots and lots of darklings. Too many.'

The women looked at each other knowingly. Aliya ducked back inside, grabbing a small pack from the peg on the wall and waving at Septimus.

'Come on,' she said.

'Who's that?' the big woman, Helga asked, braid swinging over a broad set of shoulders.

'Septimus,' Aliya said. 'He's a friend. Let's go.'

'Come along now, Elizabeth,' Helga said to a girl Septimus had not noticed. She was about his age, tall, almost as tall as him, with a long gold braid just like Helga. He could see the family resemblance, although Elizabeth did not have Helga's girth. He thought she was quite pretty, then chided himself as an idiot. *What are you doing, thinking about pretty girls at a time like this?*

He followed Aliya and Helga down the street, away from the sound of fighting that was growing louder with every second. Black smoke started to billow in the starry sky above them, its rancid smell filling the air, screams and prayers echoing through the fort as people ran. Tribby added her piercing cry to the cacophony.

'Where are we going?' Septimus asked, unsure if Aliya could even hear him. It was only then that he realised he had left his own pack behind in her house.

'The back gate,' Elizabeth puffed beside him.

He looked across and gave her a wane smile. The muddy street once again clawed at his boots, as if the very earth were trying to stop him, to hold him in place until the forces of the dark god could catch him and tear him to pieces. Panic was starting to well inside him. He recognised it, recognised that his body was responding to the stimuli around him, to the fear and desperation that was overwhelming the fort's aura. Instead of succumbing, Septimus started to recite a litany in his head, one his master had taught him to calm himself.

The Allmother loves all. It is she who watches over man, beast and plant alike. It is she who shelters us within her loving embrace, under the light of her tree. There is no fear so great within a man's heart that she cannot quell.

'The streets are blocked,' Helga said, her booming voice pulling his attention back.

Their group had stopped in the middle of the road, boots sinking into the layer of mud. Before them, a mass of people was pushing towards the rear gate, pressed together in an immovable mass as they tried to escape.

'We should –'

Screams broke out ahead of them, cutting off whatever Aliya was going to say. The crowd was breaking up, turning and trying to run in the opposite direction, straight towards them. The four of them scrambled out of the road, pressing up against the wall of a large warehouse. Shadows flickered everywhere, torches waving wildly in the grip of people who tried to flee. A building across the way somehow caught on fire, flames igniting in a whoosh, the conflagration shooting into the dark sky faster than Septimus thought was natural.

'Darklings, coming from both sides,' Aliya said.

While the defenders had been occupied with the attack on the main gates, another force of the monsters had circled the fort to attack the civilians as they fled.

'The slip hole,' Helga said.

'You have an escape tunnel?' Septimus asked. Despite his training, he had started to despair. To finally find the host of the Allmother's power, only to be trapped, the certainty of death closing in from every side was almost too much. He clung to the slim hope of escape.

'The streets are chaos, we'll never get there,' Aliya said. She made hushing noises at Tribby who was wailing on her hip.

'The rooftops,' Elizabeth said, voice almost too soft to hear.

'What?' Aliya asked.

'I can get us there along the rooftops,' the girl answered. She near bounced on her toes as she spoke, stepping out to look up at the roof of the warehouse.

Septimus looked towards the gate. The crush of people had become a tide, washing down the road, screams drowning out all but the hideous screeches of the darklings. He couldn't see them yet, but the screams were getting closer, meaning the monsters were as well. Trying to focus on the conversation, he did his best to ignore the horrific sound of innocent people being torn apart.

'Are you sure?' Aliya asked, eyes wide with fear.

'She's always clambering across the roofs,' Helga said. 'Get moving.' The big woman hiked a thumb over her shoulder.

'Wait,' Aliya said. Dropping her pack, she pulled out a bolt of cloth, wrapping it expertly around Elizabeth and tucking Tribby snuggly into it on the girls' back. 'Get moving!'

Aliya manhandled the girl before she could protest, pushing her into Helga's waiting hands. Helga already had her back braced to the wall, hand cupped on one knee. With an easy heave, she pushed her daughter up to the eaves, pushing her foot as the girl scrambled onto the slate roof.

'You're next,' Aliya said, shoving him.

Before he knew what was happening, Helga had hefted him up the wall as well. His forearms scraped painfully on the eave, tearing skin, but he clambered up with only a little assistance from Elizabeth.

'Mum!' the girl shouted.

The crowd had completely broken, the tide of darklings now mere feet away from Aliya and Helga with little to stop them.

'Protect my girl!' Aliya screamed at them.

'Run!' Helga bellowed, although whether at them or Aliya, he wasn't sure. The big woman pushed Aliya back down the street and picked up a still burning brand one of the fleeing villagers had dropped in the street. She brandished it like a club and stepped towards the approaching darklings.

Despite the burning building across the street, Septimus could barely make out the evil creatures. It was like they weren't entirely there, slipping between the light, materialising only in the darkest shadows.

'Come on,' Elizabeth shouted, yanking at his sleeve.

Septimus didn't see what happened to Aliya. He followed the girl as she sprinted across the tiles, her footing sure on the sloping roof. It took all his concentration not to fall but Elizabeth seemed perfectly comfortable. Assuming they would climb down on the other side of the building, he slowed, only to see the girl speed up and leap across the gap between the warehouse and the building next to it, boots sliding to a halt. Not thinking, Septimus sped up and launched himself. The fear hit him half-way across the gap as he looked down into the darkness below, arms windmilling as the air rushed around him.

'Keep moving,' Elizabeth hissed. Tears streaked her face and yet she moved with resolve. Tribby bounced along on her back, gurgling happily at the movement. They leapt across three more gaps, Septimus barely making the last, before she led them down onto a stack of crates and into a pitch-black alley.

'Where are we?' he asked, lungs working hard to both speak and suck in air.

'Quiet.'

There was a scratching sound and the squeak of rusty hinges. He could barely make out Elizabeth's form in the darkness, yet she moved confidently as she took his hand and pulled him forward. They descended a rough set of stairs made from wood, if the creak was anything to go by, the dank smell of wet earth surrounding them. If the night above was black, then the darkness they now found themselves in were absolute. Had it not been for the sure steps of Elizabeth and the way she gripped his hand, Septimus was sure he would have turned back, rather facing the horror of the darklings than whatever hid in the abyss they were in.

Their steps made odd thudding noises, barely an echo being made, like his senses were muted. He reached out a hand and touched dirt. They were clearly underground, in a rough-hewn tunnel. Trusting to this girl he had just met, Septimus followed. They walked for almost twenty minutes by his reckoning, never turning nor veering in the slightest.

'Watch your step.'

Elizabeth's voice made him jump.

He found himself stepping onto another set of wooden steps, this time ascending. Another squeal of rusty hinges and a breeze of cool night air blew down the tunnel around him. He let out a sigh of relief as they stepped into the night, stars twinkling softly overhead to greet him.

The girl helped him up the final step. Septimus saw that Tribby was asleep against her back, the girl's tiny face mushed into her dress, smearing drool on it. He turned at the gasp.

Elizabeth stood and looked at Fort Astral in the distance. It was burning. The smell of fire and screams of horror reached them even at this distance.

'What do we do now?' she asked through sobs, fighting back the grief that wanted to drown her in tears.

Septimus looked at her, then at Tribby. He hoped Aliya made it out alive but knew they couldn't wait to find out. His duty came first.

'We run,' he answered. 'And we protect this little girl with our lives. She is more important than you could ever imagine.'

A pack of wolves howled in the woods behind them. Elizabeth flinched beside him, but Septimus felt no fear. He knew those howls, knew that they were beckoning him to safety, that the guardians were here to protect Tribby.

'Let's go,' he said, pulling Elizabeth away and turning them towards the trees. 'We have a duty to perform.'

They trotted into the woods, fleeing from the darklings and the horrors that they brought.

About the Author

Scott Cirakovic started his descent into the sci-fi and fantasy abyss at a young age. Now, older but no more mature, he writes books about aliens and larger than life sword and sorcery heroes. He has served in the Australian Army for over fifteen year and channels the rage and caffeine addiction into compelling stories that will leave you wanting to dive into the abyss with him. Having a small-town origin story is a bit cliche, so let's just say he has been a wandering nomad across Australia but has finally settled down in Queensland with his chaos fueled family and chimera sized canines.

www.ingramcontent.com/pod-product-compliance
Lightning Source LLC
LaVergne TN
LVHW041813060526
838201LV00046B/1255